BLACKWATER
LINCOLN'S WAR IN WEST FLORIDA

BLACKWATER

LINCOLN'S WAR IN WEST FLORIDA

RICHARD KYLE SMITH

The Regency Publishers

Copyright © 2023 Richard Kyle Smith.

All rights reserved. No part of this book may be reproduced in any form or by any electronic or mechanical means, including information storage and retrieval systems, without permission in writing from the author and publisher, except by reviewers, who may quote brief passages in a review.

ISBN: 978-1-958517-33-8   (Paperback Edition)
ISBN: 978-1-958517-34-5   (Hardcover Edition)
ISBN: 978-1-958517-32-1   (E-book Edition)

Some characters and events in this book are fictitious and products of the author's imagination. Any similarity to real persons, living or dead, is coincidental and not intended by the author.

Book Ordering Information

The Regency Publishers, US
521 5th Ave 17th floor NY, NY10175

Phone Number: (315)537-3088 ext 1007
Email: info@theregencypublishers.com
www.theregencypublishers.com

Printed in the United States of America

CONTENTS

Acknowledgments xi
Author's Notes.. xiii
Introduction xv
Prologue xvii

PART 1

Chapter 1: John Geoghegan:
Running The Union Blockade, 1861--1865 3

PART II

Chapter 2: John Geoghegan: Before The War Between The States 9
Chapter 3: Jose Garcia: River Gambia 10
Chapter 4: H. R. Parry: John's Departure 13
Chapter 5: Captain Eric Skultety: Malaga To Yarmouth 16
Chapter 6: The Hanshaw Brothers: Bear River, Nova Scotia 18
Chapter 7: Captain Burt Mclocklin: Nova Scotia To Key West 24
Chapter 8: Maria Moreno: Pensacola 27
Chapter 9: The Mill Town: Milton, Florida 33
Chapter 10: Maria Sent To Spain 35
Chapter 11: John's Would-Be Captor, Oliver Watson 38
Chapter 12: Northern Hostility:
John's Lack Of Knowledge Of Moreno's Plan 40
Chapter 13: Michael Smith 41
Chapter 14: Susanna 43

Chapter 15: Moreno Apologizes 45
Chapter 16: The First Blockade Run:
            The Union Boards The Carolina 47
Chapter 17: Halloween: Thirteenth Blockade Run 50
Chapter 18: Destroying Union Frigates 53
Chapter 19: John Finds Maria 55

PART III

Chapter 20: Ben Jernigan, Jacob Rucker, Amanda Rucker 61
Chapter 21: Ben Jernigan: Waiting Out The War 65
Chapter 22: Caleb 71
Chapter 23: Clayton's Box: Trip To Milton 79
Chapter 24: Zeke: Caleb's Plan 82
Chapter 25: Ben's Trip For Guns And Ammunition 85
Chapter 26: Ben Saves Amanda 88
Chapter 27: Celeste, Escape From Milton 90
Chapter 28: Caleb Sails For Fort Pickens,
            Ben And Amanda Hideout 93
Chapter 29: Amanda's Tragedy 96
Chapter 30: Ben's Viewpoint 100
Chapter 31: Yankee Racism 102
Chapter 32: Sister Alice 103
Chapter 33: Ben Finds John 105
Chapter 34: The Rest Of John's Story 107
Chapter 35: Hernando Lopez, Jose Garcia 109
Chapter 36: Matt And Mark: Accumulating Trade Goods 114
Chapter 37: Charles W. Ware 119
Chapter 38: Going To Brazil: William Clayton's Suicide 121

Epilogue 125

This book is dedicated to the Confederate citizens,
most of whom owned no slaves,
who died when the Union invaded their homeland.

We are capable of many things in all directions of great virtues and great sins. And who, in his mind, has not probed the black water?

—**John Steinbeck**, *East of Eden*

ACKNOWLEDGMENTS

There are many people I would like to thank for their work on this book: My sister-in-law Paula Smith and Elizabeth Hamilton for their excellent typing, editing, and suggestions; Nathan Woolsy for his advice on historical matters; Carol Culton for her proofreading; as well as Mary Brewer, Caroline Thompson, and Judy Smith for reading and suggestions. Thank you to Shad Helmstetter for his publishing advice, photographer Jerry Patterson, and finally, Kim Saunders for his patient technical assistance.

There are also others who should be mentioned, but my old memory fails me. Thanks to them as well.

Richard Kyle Smith

AUTHOR'S NOTES

The historical background of *Blackwater* is essentially factual. The characters and their actions are fictional. Cedar Grove is fictional, as is the Clayton Family who lived there in the story.

I trust that my fictional account of the period depicted in the story fairly represents the hardships inflicted on the people in the Pensacola Bay area during and after the War of Southern Independence: a war that could have been avoided. Conventional wisdom has always been that the Union blockades could not be run out of Pensacola Bay. But I think not. Of course, my accounts of how it could be done are fictional.

The war for Southern Independence was not about the Union freeing the slaves. It seems few white Americans, North or South, were overly concerned about the status of the enslaved black people. As outlined here, Lincoln, disregarding the Constitution, attacked the Southern States to force them to stay in the Union. Even though the Southern States withdrew, Lincoln would not allow it. The so-called "Great Emancipator" caused hundreds of thousands of people to be killed for reasons that had nothing to do with slavery. The reasons are explained herein.

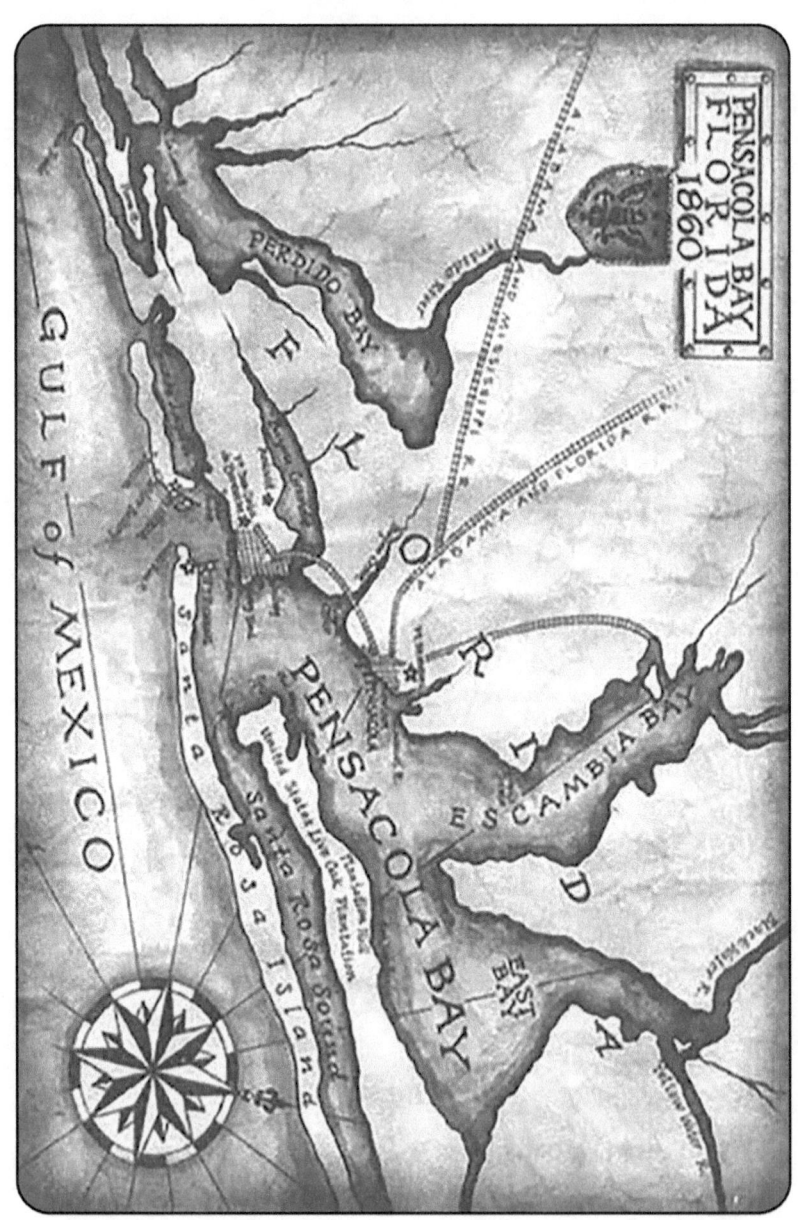

INTRODUCTION

The Pensacola Bay area was booming in 1860, primarily because of the seemingly unlimited supply of virgin yellow pines that grew from the Gulf Coast to well up into Alabama. Milton, on the Blackwater River, was the most industrialized city in Florida before the war. Lumber for building and all manner of wooden products were manufactured and exported from Northwest Florida, also known as the Florida Panhandle.

When the guns were fired at Fort Sumter, the Union army held Fort Pickens, located on the western tip of Santa Rosa Island, where it guarded access to Pensacola Bay. It allegedly eliminated Pensacola Bay as a place to run the Union blockade.

A north-south railroad was recently built from Pensacola, going north to Montgomery, Alabama, and beyond. Union general Ulysses S. Grant was advancing his army into Western Tennessee and had to be stopped. Confederate general Braxton Bragg had about 5,000 Confederate soldiers in Pensacola. So it was decided by the Confederate secretary of war not only to leave the Pensacola Bay area defenseless by sending Bragg's army to Tennessee but also to initiate a scorched earth policy for the entire bay area. This was to prevent anything valuable from falling into the hands of the Union. General Bragg and his troops took the last train out of Pensacola (taking the rails up behind them to the Alabama line). After the Confederacy withdrew, most of the citizens went north to the relative safety of South Alabama. However, some petitioned the Union army for protection when Pensacola fell into Union hands. The Western Panhandle became a "no-man's-land." A few stayed, and this tale is about some of them.

PROLOGUE

Before the War Between the States, affluent ladies and gentlemen of the city of Pensacola would sometimes be ferried from the mainland in the cool of the day to the sugar-fine white- sand beaches of Santa Rosa Island. The ladies would stand facing the surf in their long, full skirts and wide-brimmed hats in the late afternoon, silhouetted against the setting sun. Their children would play in the water or build sand castles. Salty breezes swept over them, carrying the aroma of the sea. Gulls cried as they hung motionless overhead. The waves pursued their ceaseless grasping for the shore. Later, the dog flies would blow in from the north and the pleasure of the moment would be gone.

PART 1

CHAPTER 1

JOHN GEOGHEGAN: RUNNING THE UNION BLOCKADE, 1861--1865

John had his own way of doing things. He and his crew slipped his ship, the *Carolina*, out of her hiding place up a deep bayou in the thick forest south of the burned-out towns of Milton and Bagdad on a night when there would be no moon. John's ship was painted black with black sails. She moved into Blackwater River, heading south. As the river widened to form the bay, friends with lanterns kept the *Carolina* in the channel. She quickly moved from Blackwater Bay into Pensacola Bay. John was then a bit more confident about the depth of the water.

He had to cross the bay at a speed that would move the ship within an area where he could see a signal from Fort Pickens--- one lantern light to proceed, two if he should abort, or three if he should hold steady because a Union ship was too close to the mouth of the harbor.

If he got the proceed signal, he had to find the channel as only he knew how. John could see the lantern light. Only one--- therefore, proceed! John was always at the wheel on these occasions. He finessed the ship around the western end of Santa Rosa Island, where Fort Pickens was guarding the harbor.

He was close enough to the fort to see Union soldiers warming themselves by a fire on this cold January night. But the soldiers could not see the ship through the early-morning blackness.

The *Carolina* moved into the gulf. John was reading his compass by a candle well hidden on the deck near the wheel. He knew in what direction he needed to go to avoid running aground. John could see a blockader moving east away from them. No other ships were visible. Fortunately, there was a north wind behind them. John waited until the *Carolina* was several miles into the gulf before he started the steam engine that powered the screw propellers. To hear the steam engine and propellers was a comforting sound.

Now, the crew replaced the black sails with white and ran up a Mexican flag. The crew started painting white on the top four feet outside the ship. It was amazing how fast they executed these tasks.

John had a highly motivated crew. They were made up entirely of men of Spanish descent, left over from when the Florida Panhandle belonged to Spain. They all spoke both Spanish and English. The reason was that if they were ever approached or boarded by a Union vessel's crew, his crew would converse in Spanish while John hid below. In the unlikely event a Union sailor could speak Spanish, he certainly could not tell the difference between Mexican Spanish and West Florida Spanish. John was prepared.

He rehearsed this useful but seemingly unlikely scenario with his crew before every mission just to be prepared. First, they would always speak rapidly in case the federal sailor's grasp of Spanish was not very good. They would laugh and look puzzled when the sailor tried to speak Spanish.

If the crew was confronted by someone proficient in Spanish, they had elaborate maps, plans, and documents to confirm the legitimacy of their journey---where they came from and other helpful information to deceive the Northerners. If their location was inconsistent with their course, they had a story of privateers or Confederates pursuing them, causing the ship to be off course. Their last action, if all else failed, would be to kill the intruders and try to escape. This cost John plenty because the crew was well rewarded if the mission was a success, but so was John.

The War between the States was not John's war. He arrived in West Florida a few years before the war began. He was a wanted man. The Royal Navy offered a five-hundred-pound reward for information leading to his arrest. John knew he would probably be found guilty, though, in reality, the facts did not support a guilty verdict. So he was trying to avoid being arrested. After the incident leading to John's predicament, he made his way to Nova Scotia and the Florida Panhandle.

He became financially independent before the war, shipping lumber and products made from wood and cotton. Then he would import whatever was ordered by his Florida Panhandle customers. So John's business was the same, but now it was more exciting.

John did not like slavery, and he did not ever own or rent a slave. It was ironic for the United States to have ever condoned slavery yet, declare that all men are created equal. He thought it amusing that Southern preachers supported slavery mightily with Bible text. He realized he was ambivalent about supporting the South but detesting slavery and even more so considering what the Confederate army had done to the Pensacola Bay area. When he was honest with himself, he knew he did it for the money and excitement.

John knew that running the blockade at Pensacola lay somewhere between highly improbable and impossible over any prolonged period. He knew that sooner or later, his luck would run out.

PART II

CHAPTER 2

JOHN GEOGHEGAN: BEFORE THE WAR BETWEEN THE STATES

John Geoghegan was born in Ireland, in County Clare, within a day's walk of the Cliffs of Moher. His father, Abraham, was the owner and captain of a merchant ship that sailed across the Atlantic to the U.S. eastern seaports. His mother was a beautiful woman named Virginia, nicknamed Ginger. She had long red hair that hung to her waist when not pinned up. When John was thirteen, his mother gave birth to a girl they named Anne. In that same year, they moved to Liverpool, so John's father would not have to travel so far on the few occasions he could spend time at home. When John was fifteen, he went to sea on his father's ship, aptly named *Ginger*. He continued his education under his father's tutelage. His father taught him seamanship as well. John was quick to learn and was well trained and educated.

Ginger, having much time to herself and with Anne, took an interest in the Anglican church and converted from Roman Catholicism to the Church of England. When Abraham and John were home, she also persuaded them to convert.

When John was twenty years old, he enlisted in the Royal Navy. He believed he would advance rapidly because of his knowledge, and experience. Within an unprecedented seven years, he was promoted to commander, a position second to the captain. He was assigned to HMS *Cook* to search out and capture ships engaged in the illegal slave trade on the Atlantic, primarily between West Africa and the West Indies. HMS *Cook* and its crew were highly successful, while Captain Nathan Woolsey was in command.

CHAPTER 3

JOSE GARCIA: RIVER GAMBIA

John was assigned the mission of going ashore on the banks of the River Gambia, a British Crown colony, with a well-armed group of riflemen and interpreters to talk to the tribal chiefs who were selling their captives from tribal warfare into slavery. John was to make it clear that explosive mines would be set in the River Gambia estuary. John was to make it understood that mining of the river could be avoided if tribal chiefs would not sell any more captives to slave traders. In exchange for their cooperation, the shipping lanes would not be mined, and certain valuable material benefits would accrue to the various tribes from the British government. Finally, John was to convey that it would be considered an act of treason by the British government if any more slave ships were encountered at sea, and it was determined that the ship came from the River Gambia.

Over a period of a couple of weeks, John and his entourage moved through the area, met, and talked with most of the chiefs, knowing that the others would get the word.

As they were making their way back to the ship, they encountered twelve large rowboats, all pulled ashore and turned upside down. John instinctively thought, *Ambush!* He immediately gave the order: "Riflemen, prepare to fire on the overturned boats!" The boats suddenly began to rise from the opposite side. The riflemen took their positions and aimed at the boats. Heads and rifles suddenly appeared from behind the boats and started to fire. But trying to fire and reload while holding up the heavy boats didn't work, so John's fifty riflemen, even without the cover, had the advantage. The attempted ambush was a failure. John's expert marksmen fired by turns and shot their targets in the head. Finally, the ambushers dropped the boats and knelt on the ground behind them. That made it difficult to load without being exposed. Some of them ran but were easily shot from behind. It was a massacre. Some of them took off their shirts and waved them to surrender; those with handkerchiefs intensely waved them. Of the forty-nine combatants, only eight were left to surrender. John called, "Cease fire." The defeated eight all came together in a group on the shore. All had abandoned their weapons and had their hands in the air.

"Who can speak for this group?" John asked.

The group was made up of white men except for one Latino. All were quiet. "What is your name?" he asked the Latino.

"I am Jose Garcia," the man replied.

"Señor Garcia, why are you in Gambia?" John inquired.

"We lost our ship *Cape Town*, in a storm last year. So we have taken up residence here while our shipwrights are building a new ship."

"You are lying. You are slavers," John said matter-of-factly. "Why did you try to ambush us?"

"We were afraid and merely trying to defend ourselves," Jose answered.

Since no British troops had even been wounded, John felt blessed.

"We have no accommodations on the ship for prisoners. Therefore, we will have to kill the rest of you," John said, feigning indifference.

Garcia spoke up. "Señor, let me make a suggestion. Why can't we put the matter into God's hands by having a duel between you and me? The winner will decide whether the prisoners are shot or released after signing an oath of loyalty to Royal British law."

John, always delighted by a challenge, quickly said, "Very well!" After the pistols were properly loaded and the rules agreed upon, the two men lined up back to back. They were to walk ten paces, counted off by a third person, turn, and fire the single-shot pistols at will. All went as planned. The men walked the ten paces and turned. Garcia fired first. John had turned sideways to make himself a smaller target. Garcia's shot missed John's vital organs and blood vessels but hit him in his left upper arm, passing through the muscle and out the back of his arm. Garcia stood waiting for the end. John aimed carefully for the middle of Jose's chest. He then saw a vulture circling overhead, which he dropped from the sky with his shot.

"You may make the decision, Señor Garcia," John said softly. Garcia said, "Release the prisoners."

John added, "Release the prisoners after they have signed the oath."

Jose Garcia came over to John and bowed to him. "Señor John, thank you for sparing my life," he said gratefully.

John nodded and said, "Do the same for someone else some time, and the next time you plan an ambush, practice it a couple of times." John, with his relatively small wound, washed with whiskey and dressed, saw to it that Garcia's group departed with limited weapons and ammunition. They headed across the Gambia River. John thought that was the last time he would encounter Jose Garcia.

CHAPTER 4

H. R. PARRY: JOHN'S DEPARTURE

H. R. Parry, a naval officer of little importance other than being an aristocrat, caused John's trouble with English authorities. Parry came across a letter while prowling furtively through Royal Navy admiral James Black's house when there as a guest. Admiral Black held the highest rank in the British navy. The letter was from John Holland, a member of the House of Lords. It setforth Black and Holland's secret love for one another and describes how they made love in the heather of the Scottish highlands.

Parry discreetly made it known to Admiral Black, through his solicitor, Lord Compton, that he had the letter and pledged discretion. This created an unspoken relationship between the two gentlemen, with Parry being the beneficiary. Admiral Black immediately made Parry the captain of the HMS *Cook,* a behemoth of the Royal British fleet, commissioned to combat and end the slave trade.

Admiral Black invited Captain Parry to his residence to celebrate his promotion. After dinner, over brandy and cigars, while their wives were absent, Parry passed the letter to the admiral. Neither mentioned the transaction. They continued their nautical conversation while the admiral tossed the letter into the flames of a nearby fireplace. The matter was closed.

John Geoghegan was coincidentally second in command of HMS *Cook*.

Parry, with his new unearned power and prestige, became a tyrant. He belittled the crew, including the officers. He would have them do unnecessary work and force many of them to wait on him, except those he was intimidated by. Parry left John alone and was never asked to bring him afternoon tea or see that his boots were polished.

Parry disagreed with ending the slave trade, which he and his ship were commissioned to accomplish. In fact, it was rumored that he himself had invested a considerable amount in that wretched endeavor. That, of course, was dismissed by Admiral Black as vicious gossip among the naval officers who were overlooked for the position of captain of the HMS *Cook*.

H. R. Parry was a consummate racist, the worst of the worst. When his ship captured a slave ship, instead of unchaining the Africans, he left them in chains on the return trip to western Africa. He allowed them one meal a day. John grew increasingly angry as he witnessed Parry's unnecessarily cruel treatment of the Africans.

Then after overtaking and capturing a large three-masted slave ship, John saw Captain Parry talking to the slave traders. He saw one of the slave traders go below deck on the slave ship and return with two filthy but attractive young black women rubbing their wrists where the chains had been. On Parry's instructions, they were washed clean with buckets of seawater. The women were taken aboard the HMS *Cook* to entertain Captain Parry.

A short time later, without Parry knowing, John saw the captain of the slave ship pass an envelope to Parry. Then Captain Parry made an announcement to the officers and crew. "There has been a mistake made here. These men are not slave traders. They were private contractors commissioned by the British government to return slaves to Africa. Release their vessel."

John stepped forward and said loudly, "Do not obey that order. Captain Parry is lying."

Parry turned red and started to sweat. "Follow my order and arrest Mr. Geoghegan."

"Captain Parry, please remove the envelope from your left coat pocket," said John.

Parry was not about to reveal the payoff from the slavers. The officers and crew stood, watched, and did not obey Parry's order. The slave traders were beginning to fidget. Parry figured his only hope was to try to kill John. Parry drew his pistol and fired at John from about fifteen feet. John dove into the deck to his right. The third officer,

Rodney Huffman, pitched John a pistol. John waited until Captain Parry reloaded. John stood sideways, waiting. Parry and John fired simultaneously. Parry fell. John did not. Parry had a hole in the middle of his forehead, visible as he lay face up with his eyes open. John ordered two officers to guard the slave traders as he closed Parry's eyes and retrieved an envelope from his coat. It contained $1,000 in U.S. currency.

John ordered that all slaves be unchained, organized into groups by region or tribe, furnished sufficient food and water, and plenty of buckets and rope to retrieve seawater for baths. Further, he put Third Officer Rodney Huffman in charge of returning the Africans, maintaining order, and sailing the confiscated three-masted ship to England.

John knew he was justified in his actions against Parry. However, unless he could prove otherwise, in the eyes of British law, he had committed mutiny and murder. He could not prove that the $1,000 on Parry was from the slave traders. Further, a captain firing a weapon at a mutineer would be considered justified, precluding a claim of self-defense. And even the fact that the slave ship was sailing in the wrong direction could be explained as a course correction. He had no knowledge of the British government using private ships to return slaves. However, it was possible. Further, John thought that the Royal Navy must hold Parry in high regard for him to have been promoted to captain of HMS Cook so soon. John also believed that Parry, being an aristocrat, would prejudice his accusers. Finally, John thought it would be a case of being guilty until proven innocent in a mutiny case since this was such a serious charge. It could take months or years to resolve the matter, and John thought the confinement and uncertainty would be unbearable. The crew would be his allies, and none of the other officers had even suggested wrongdoing on his part. John made his decision. He would sail to Gibraltar, and from there, he would make his way to Nova Scotia.

When HMS *Cook* reached Gibraltar, he assembled his officers and the entire crew. He assigned the second officer as acting captain and resigned from his commission. He then thanked them for their support, said his goodbyes, and departed. Thereafter, he called himself John Smith.

CHAPTER 5

CAPTAIN ERIC SKULTETY: MALAGA TO YARMOUTH

From Gibraltar, John went to Malaga. From there, he was drawn to a shipping company he noticed because of its name, Skultety. John went in, met with the owners, and persuaded them to engage his services as temporary captain of the *Del Sol* and move him toward Nova Scotia.

His contract required him to take the ship to Valencia and Barcelona to pick up cork and produce and take them to Cardiff, Wales. After the cork and produce were unloaded, he was to take coal to Reykjavik, Iceland. He was to refuel in Cardiff and again at the port of Bergen, Norway, before crossing over to Reykjavik. His Spanish vessel was a two-stack oceangoing side wheeler.

All went well until he reached Bergen. There, after refueling, he and some of the other crew members went to a tavern. He picked up enough of the conversation in Norwegian to understand that all the dogs, cats, and free-range domesticated animals were gone and were thought to have moved to higher elevations. John warned the people in the tavern that a tsunami was coming and that they should warn everyone to seek higher ground. Some laughed, and some did as John suggested.

Then John asked, "Where is there a fjord that is deep and parallel to the ocean?"

An old man named Eric Skultety, perhaps eighty-five years old, said, "Several miles up from here. May I join you?"

"Thanks, of course," John replied.

John hurriedly explained their plight to the crew. So they quickly cast off and turned and headed inland up the fjord.

After what seemed like an eternity, Skultety, who had a full white beard, said, "There it is, on the port side."

John nodded and entered the fjord. Before John fully entered the side fjord, he looked to the left and saw a wall of water moving toward them from about two miles away. Then, as they entered, he saw nothing but the wall of the side fjord. John could no longer see the tsunami but could hear its roar.

After going a quarter of a mile up the fjord, John ordered, "Drop anchors," followed by, "Go below deck and secure the hatches!"

The tsunami rumbled and splashed through the main fjord. When it reached the side fjord where the *Del Sol* was secured, the current banked on the inside wall of the side fjord and raised the water level for a few minutes until it had been elevated, perhaps seventy-five feet. It did no damage to the vessel. Then as the seawater began to recede swiftly, John pushed the steam engines and went to full speed to resist being pulled out of the side fjord. It worked! The entire affair didn't last more than an hour and a half. "We shall wait here until we know if more waves are coming." They waited two days and then sailed out of the fjords and back into the Norwegian Sea. The Norwegian Sea was rough but nothing like a tsunami. If the *Del Sol* had been in the open sea, she would have been ripped to pieces. John had saved the ship owners a considerable amount of money. Then he thought about Skultety, who helped him. He forgot to drop him off in Bergen. He went hunting for him, and when he found him, he was asleep in a bunk, midship. John woke him. While John had a serious look on his face as the old man aroused, smiling a broad smile.

"Don't worry, John, I'm Captain Skultety. I own the company. I'll sail with you to Reykjavik, then to Yarmouth, pick up some cargo, and return the *Del Sol* to Spain. John, you saved the *Del Sol*. To show our gratitude, I will send $1,000 to your bank in Annapolis Royal when I get back to Malaga."

As it turned out, Eric Skultety had been on the *Del Sol* since it sailed from Malaga to keep an eye on John.

CHAPTER 6

THE HANSHAW BROTHERS: BEAR RIVER, NOVA SCOTIA

John made it to the seaport town of Yarmouth, Nova Scotia, in two months, arriving in early winter. Hitching wagon rides, he traveled up Annapolis Road, where a side road led to Bear River. John thanked the man who had given him a ride to the Bear River turnoff, unloaded his few belongings, and started walking toward his destination. The temperature was well below freezing, and John was used to the tropics. He walked several miles in the dreary late afternoon half-light in snow up to his ankles. John was miserably cold and had second thoughts about choosing this godforsaken place to hide. Just as darkness began closing around him, John saw the light from a campfire about a hundred feet off on the left side of the road.

He could hear someone playing harmonica.

John stumbled his way down the gentle incline of a seldom-trod path to a clearing. The fire drew him like a moth, but he did not want to startle the two men he saw there. They were sitting on a log under a canvas shelter with the fire blazing in front of them.

From a respectful distance, John called to them. "Nice fire. Mind if I join you?"

The harmonica music stopped, and the men looked out through the dancing shadows cast by the campfire. The larger of the two men stood. After sizing John up, he replied, "No, help yourself."

John moved in slowly and stood by the fire. He unbuttoned his coat and held it open, letting the warmth penetrate his chilled-to-the-bone body. "Thanks. Name's John Smith. Tryin' to get to Bear River."

"I'm Matt Hanshaw, and this is my brother, Mark. You got people in Bear River? We're kin to just about everybody there." Mark stood up, smiling and nodding a greeting.

"Nope, I'm lookin' for work," John said.

"Bout the only work around Bear River is cutting timber," Matt offered.

"Any sawmill work or carpentering?" John asked.

"A little, not much. Most of that work is taken, kinda inherited, you might say."

By this time, Mark had started cooking supper over the fire, which had matured into orange glowing logs radiating heat and crackling quietly. The sky started spitting tiny, almost dry beads of snow, which evaporated over the fire, lightly powdering the three men.

"Where you from?" Mark asked when things got quiet for a moment.

"Ireland. Been a ship's carpenter." John had actually been a ship's carpenter briefly on HMS *Cook* on his way up the ranks. "I got tired of the rockin' of the water and decided to try land for a while."

"Why, of all places, did you pick Bear River to look for work?" Mark asked with a puzzled expression.

"I met a fellow from there once. I can't remember his name, but he made it sound like a nice place to live." John was getting tired of questions.

"He must have been away a long time. I wonder why if he liked it that much, he ever left," Mark said.

"You can ride to town with us tomorrow," Matt offered, changing the subject. "And you can share our supper and shelter tonight if you like."

"I'd be very grateful," said John.

"We were hoping to shoot us a deer in the morning," said Matt as he put a few dry oak limbs on the fire. He brought out a fruit jar with an amber-colored liquid in it. The three men passed the jar, each taking a few small swallows, and John found it to be good home-distilled whiskey. After Matt gave thanks, they ate bacon and potatoes, cleaned the utensils, and turned in for the night. A few minutes later, they were all asleep. Later, the snow stopped falling. The woods were white and silent.

John awoke suddenly the following morning to the sound of a gunshot. Matt and Mark had left their bedrolls early and gone hunting.

About thirty minutes later, they appeared with a six-point buck hanging from a pole they carried at each end.

"Good morning," they said almost in unison. It was apparent they were pleased with their success. Within a short time, they had the deer hanging from a tree limb and were busily engaged in field-dressing it.

"Nice buck," John said.

Matt and Mark continued the grizzly task. John had built a fire and started cooking breakfast after he awoke, assuming it would take them a while to return with their kill. After breakfast, they hitched up their mule, loaded the wagon, and made the trip to Bear River.

The Hanshaw brothers saw to it that John was well taken care of by introducing him around town, finding him a boardinghouse, and they took him on to do contract logging with them.

Matt was the older and larger of the two, built like John but light-complexioned and about an inch taller. Mark was three years younger than Matt and of medium build. Despite the difference in size, it was easy to tell that the Hanshaws were brothers. They had a great sense of humor and constantly tried to outdo one another with practical jokes. On one occasion, Mark loosely secured the mules to the wagon. When Matt got on the wagon and slapped the reins, the mules took off without the wagon, and so did Matt! Matt got even later by painstakingly collecting fleas off one of the mules' blankets, putting them into a jar, and emptying them into Mark's bedroll.

Matt liked to talk about the two years he spent sailing out of Halifax with his uncle, Captain John Hanshaw. But the brothers lost their father in a logging accident, and their mother had no way to support herself. Mark was only seventeen at that time and couldn't make enough money by himself, so Matt reluctantly came home. That's when they started the timber business. Their mother died three years later. By then, the brothers were established in logging. Matt continued to dream of going back to the sea or at least leaving Bear River.

The three men worked well together and had a good time, both at work and on weekends in town. They'd have a few drinks on Saturday night and go to church together on Sunday. Since their names represented three of the four Gospels, they jokingly started referring to each other as Brother Matt, Brother Mark, and Brother John. The only contact they had with young ladies was at church socials and infrequently at dances in the lodge building across from the tavern.

A city girl came, visiting relatives the first summer John was there. Mark showed her around Bear River and secretly took her for a walk in the woods. After she left, Mark kept a smile on his face for a month but never revealed to John and Matt what had happened.

The following winter, Captain Frederick Berry, out of Halifax, had taken leave of his merchant ship to visit Bear River, his boyhood home. He entertained the locals with stories of his adventures on the Atlantic. He also told of his desire to eventually settle in a warmer climate. He mentioned Pensacola and Milton as a possibility. "And there is plenty of work there, in timber and sawmilling." This appealed to John, Matt, and Mark, especially on this particular night when the temperature was five degrees outside. Captain Berry departed after a few weeks, but his words lingered with the three men.

After much deliberation, Matt and Mark decided there was nothing keeping them in Bear River except an almost subsistence living in the logging business, so they determined to make their way south. John was reluctant to leave because of his fear of being recognized and apprehended by the authorities. He knew a sketch of him had probably been distributed to law enforcement agencies in the United States, as well as in Europe. Without seriously explaining why, John told the Hanshaws' that he planned to stay in Bear River. "I love the weather here," he just said.

John stood as the sun began to rise on a hill overlooking the tiny village of Bear River. Well-kept wooden houses and two white steepled churches clung to the hillsides on each side of the stream that gave the place its name. A steep dirt road serving as the main street stretched down to a small wooden bridge over the river. An ancient dam-and-water-powered mill stood just downstream on John's side of the divide. That was about all there was to Bear River, Nova Scotia.

John had lived in a small boardinghouse near where he now stood. The Hanshaws' logging business had provided him with a roof over his head and three meals a day but little else. After he left the British navy, he had considered this backwoods village a safe place to hide from the British authorities, at least until the passions his actions had aroused subsided. Like what he told the Hanshaw brothers, he had heard about

Bear River from a mellowed-out seaman in a bar in Liverpool. It was the seaman's boyhood home, and under the influence of too much warm grog, he made it sound like the most wonderful place on earth. He had endured two winters in Nova Scotia and didn't look forward to another.

September brought the blazing fall colors of the sugar maples. This announced that soon, the neatly cut and stacked firewood that adorned the back porches of the village residents would be manifesting itself as clouds of smoke from their chimneys. The frigid air would send the migrating birds south before the snow came.

John thought that perhaps it was time for him to migrate as well. He went for a walk through the cemetery on the hill above the village and thought of home. He wondered about his mother and father. Were they still living? If so, were they in good health? Were they upset that he had not written them? Or did they understand that it was too dangerous? He believed they understood.

What had become of his younger sister? Is she married by now? She could have her pick from amongst almost any eligible young men who had ever met her. She was that desirable. Tears came to his eyes when he thought how much he missed his family. Then he decided. Yes, he would leave this place. Before he did, he would write them a long letter expressing his love for them and explaining the terrible events at sea that forced him into hiding. By the time his letter could be traced, he would be long departed from Bear River.

Meanwhile, the Hanshaws' were saying their goodbyes to family and friends, and they were taxied toward Annapolis Road by a friend with a wagon and four mules. About two miles out of Bear River, the Hanshaw boys were surprised and delighted to see John Smith walking out of the woods.

"Can you give me a lift?" John said with a teasing smile on his face. Matt, the older of the two boys, jumped down from the wagon, grabbed John by the seat of his pants, and threw him into the open rear of the wagon. Mark, the younger Hanshaw, fetched his bag and hurled it into the wagon.

"Hope there wasn't anything breakable in there," Mark yelled.

"Oh, just a hundred-year-old bottle of single-malt scotch," John said in a deadpan fashion.

After a long, bumpy ride, they reached Annapolis on the Bay of Fundy. The tide was out, and the mudflats seemed to run on forever. It was a sunny morning, and to John, Matt, and Mark, the contrast between the sunny openness here and the grim forest at Bear River was breathtaking.

When the tide came back in, the trio made arrangements to ride out on it when it retreated again. They found a derelict skiff boat that looked like it would float even though it had obviously been abandoned and had a greatly needed pair of old oars left in it.

Though the small boat had no visible holes, they knew it would leak badly, so they went to the mercantile and bought two buckets. The plan was to have Matt, the biggest and strongest, row while John and Mark bailed. They pushed the boat from the bank into the water and rowed out about fifty yards. The leaking, bailing, and rowing seemed to be working. All of a sudden, they felt the boat being pulled faster and faster away from shore toward the ships anchored far enough out in deep water that they could resist the tidal flow in and out of the bay.

CHAPTER 7

CAPTAIN BURT MCLOCKLIN: NOVA SCOTIA TO KEY WEST

It was almost dark when they reached the first anchored vessel. "Ahoy!" John cried out. "Where are you bound, and what is your cargo?" John didn't want to board a ship unless he knew its cargo was legal. An arrest would be dangerous to him because of his past misadventure.

A New England accent called back, "We are bound for Savannah, and our cargo will be maple syrup."

"When will you sail?"

"Tomorrow," the reply came back.

"Can you use three able-bodied hands?"

"Pay or passage?" the disembodied voice asked.

"Pay and passage," John offered.

"Passage," came the reply.

"Passage and meals," John negotiated.

"Done, come aboard," said the invisible benefactor.

The pilgrims abandoned their barely worthy boat to the vicissitudes of Fundy.

All night long, they loaded maple syrup in the ship's hold. By morning, the ship was loaded, and John, Matt, and Mark were exhausted. The captain of the vessel was a rail-thin New Englander of about six feet and seventy years. He was stern in appearance, but something about him gave John the impression that the sternness was fake and that he could drop that façade at any moment. He griped about how slowly John and the others had been working the night before. But after the ship weighed anchor, he invited them to the captain's table to eat breakfast.

"And where are you landlubbers from?" he asked, not realizing that John and Mark had spent much time on the water as he had.

"Bear River," answered Mark.

"And where the hell is that?" the captain replied.

"In the woods a few miles from here," Mark responded.

"Perhaps we should introduce ourselves," John said to create more of an air of civility.

"This is Matt Hanshaw and his brother Mark, and I am John Smith."

"John Smith." The captain smiled. "I've met a lot of John Smiths. Couldn't you be a little more original?"

John thought about it and said "yep" and said no more.

"Well, I'm Burt McLocklin," the captain said. He immediately got up and went below.

McLocklin had planned several ports of call, and fortunately, Pensacola was one of them. The weather was favorable, so they had a good time. The first city they dropped anchor was Savannah. After having sized up Matt, Mark, and John, Captain Mclocklin announced to the crew that the Hanshaw boys and John Smith would stand the first watch. "Thereafter, I'll have a new list posted with departure date and time included. Don't get in jail because nobody's gonna post bond for you, and damn it, don't pick up anything from them whores. If you ain't here to sail on time, we'll leave your asses."

Then Captain McLocklin got a big grin on his face and walked down the gangplank toward a beautiful dark-haired woman in her mid-fifties waving at him.

"Must be his daughter," Mark said.

"Not likely," John opined, trying to keep a straight face. Matt busted out laughing.

Although the ship's accommodations and food were not very good, the weather was. The vessel made good time, but still, it seemed the trip took forever. John spent most of his time reading his precious books, including the King James Version of the Bible. He had always loved books, so the trip passed faster for him than for Matt and Mark. Matt and Mark liked to watch the dolphins traveling alongside the ship and the occasional whales swimming lazily nearby, spouting water that looked like steam from a distance.

They sailed around the Florida peninsula and stopped briefly in Key West for rest and entertainment. After a week, Captain McLocklin announced they would sail for Pensacola the following morning. This, of course, upset the crew and their Key West girlfriends, at least until the crew reached Pensacola and the Key West girls met the crew of another ship.

CHAPTER 8

MARIA MORENO: PENSACOLA

A few days later, the Northwest Florida coast came into view. They were amazed at the whiteness of the sandy beaches. They were much whiter than those on the East Coast. They went into the harbor past the inactive Fort Pickens, crossed Pensacola Bay, and docked at the wharf.

After an afternoon of sightseeing, they found rooms for the night. They went out for the evening and found Pensacola to be a lively place. They came upon a group of men speaking Spanish. John knew Spanish and began to enter into their conversation. After a few minutes, he walked over to Matt and Mark and said, "Come on." They followed the Spaniards to a saloon off Palafox Street, a few blocks from the docks. The place was filled with seamen from the ships in port; many were Hispanics and a few Anglos. They spoke several different languages but predominately Spanish. They were a congenial group for the most part. The music was lively Latin, and a few couples were dancing to the tune of a small Spanish band.

John, Matt, and Mark sat at the bar with their new Spanish acquaintances who were trying to teach the Hanshaw boys a few useful words of Spanish. There was a relatively large number of women in the saloon, and John suspected that most unescorted women were there to make money.

Across the room, John's eyes met the eyes of a beautiful Spanish girl. They gazed at each other for a moment, both smiling, and then she looked away. She was sitting with a rough-looking white man whose company she didn't seem to care for. He seemed to be trying to get her to dance with him, and she appeared to be saying no. She suddenly glanced back at John with pleading eyes, and that was all it took. John walked over to where she was seated and said in Spanish, "It's time we go now." She nodded, got up, and walked out the door with him. Something about him made her trust him.

Once outside, he said, "Allow me to introduce myself. My name is John Smith." He spoke in Spanish.

She said in English, "I am Maria Moreno."

They both smiled at their first conversation.

"Let's use English," she said. John nodded. "My uncle would kill me for being here. My sister Alvina and I wanted an adventure. But the first time a man offered to buy Alvina a drink, she lost her nerves and left me."

John could see her under the lamplight above them. Maria had an appealing voice and an even more appealing appearance with her smooth olive skin, bright brown eyes, and black hair. She had a perfectly petite figure and a beautiful smile. Wearing a white peasant blouse pulled slightly off her shoulders and a full red skirt with matching sandals, she could turn any man's head.

"Thank you for helping me. Maybe I will see you again next Sunday afternoon in the park." After she rushed off up Palafox Street, John realized that she had subtly requested that they meet again. She was, he thought, the most beautiful and desirable girl he had ever met.

When John went back inside, the man Maria left at the table looked him up and down. But he had consumed a great deal of rum and was not in the mood or in any condition to confront him. In another hour, his head was resting on the table.

Matt and Mark and their newfound friends were not making much progress with their Spanish lessons, but after a few rounds of rum, they didn't care. They were now conversing in English, telling wild tales to one another, mostly lies.

John had two pints of ale and a large plate of fried mullet and was ready for bed. John gathered up Matt and Mark. They all said good night to their new friends Ricardo, Michel, and Juan. They then headed back to their rooms, Matt and Mark a bit wobbly. It was Friday night.

Saturday, they all slept in. Matt and Mark were sleeping off rum hangovers, and John was just enjoying sleeping on land again. The accommodations, though sparse, were much better than those on the ship.

On Sunday, after cleaning up and dressing, he left the Hanshaw boys asleep and went to an early service at Christ Episcopal Church but left before the service started and inquired where Maria Moreno's family attended church. A lady entering the church gave him a knowing look and a conspiratorial smile as she directed him up Palafox Street a few blocks. He hurried up the street and found St. Michael's Catholic Church. He entered and walked down the aisle to what looked to be an unspoken-for pew. He knelt, made the sign of the cross, and sat down. A few rows in front of him, he saw the back of Maria's head. His heart started to pound.

After the service ended, he smiled at Maria when she noticed him. She smiled back. He knew that the large contingent seated together had to be her family and that the distinguished older gentleman must be her uncle Don Francisco Moreno, a well- known and respected citizen of Pensacola. Burt McLocklin had told John that Moreno was extremely wealthy and had financed his ship. John walked up to the gentleman he thought to be Maria's uncle and very politely said in his best Spanish, "Señor Moreno? May I introduce myself?" Then he waited politely.

"Of course, please do," Señor Moreno said in English, realizing by his appearance that these must be John's first few days in Pensacola. "Welcome, and how may I be of service to you?"

"I am John Smith. My partners and I would like to go into business in the timber trades, and we thought perhaps you could advise us. We were referred by Captain McLocklin."

"Well, you will find the weather more agreeable here---that is, if you can avoid the fever. Stay away from the swamps as much as possible," Moreno advised. "Why don't you join us for a picnic at Seville Square this noon? We can mix business with pleasure."

"You are so kind," John responded. "I accept."

During the afternoon of the picnic, John talked business with Señor Moreno and was introduced to dozens of relatives and friends of Don Francisco Moreno but not to Maria. Finally, a group of young people came walking up, and Señor Moreno began introducing them as his nephews and nieces, the children of his deceased brother Don Carlos. Maria was among them, holding the hand of Angela, the youngest daughter of Don Francisco Moreno. Maria winked at John without anyone noticing. Señor Moreno spent a long time petting and talking about Angela. She was a beautiful ten-year-old child and obviously his favorite. After talking business for a couple of hours, John asked Señor Moreno for permission to take Maria on a walk so that she could show him the city. He hesitated but then consented. Chaperones were a thing of the past on this frontier.

"Be back before dark," Señor Moreno yelled as an afterthought when they were a block away.

"My uncle said you are interested in the timber industry, perhaps starting a business. There is much competition. Perhaps you should consider some other business. Shipping the processed lumber is always profitable if you make the right connections." It was apparent that Maria did not want John to get discouraged and move away.

"I could be gone for months shipping lumber," John noted.

"But you would come back. I might not see you again if you get into the Alabama woods." Oh no, she had revealed her heart. "What I mean is, you can do well-shipping timber out of Pensacola and Milton, and we can still see each other."

They were in a secluded spot under a three-hundred-year-old live oak tree with long limbs that drooped to the ground. John kissed her, and Maria kissed him just as enthusiastically. They kissed and embraced until the sun began to set, and Maria remembered her uncle's words. "I must get back so we can do this again," she said as she smiled.

Then she nestled her head against his chest, ran her hand down his body, and felt his hardness. She then said, "I am a virgin, and someday I want you to be the man to have me."

She then dashed off to catch up with her family. John savored the moment---the slight chill of the early November evening, the salty smell of the bay nearby, the distant cry of the seagulls, and what Maria had just said and done.

John, at first, could think about nothing but Maria. Then he thought about what she had said. She wanted him. Her idea to ship lumber made good sense as well. Lumber was pouring in from the hinterlands and sitting on the docks waiting to be shipped. He could leave the backbreaking work of lumberjacking and sawmilling to others and simply transport the finished product to wherever it was needed.

Still, the problem was acquiring financing for a ship. He knew how to sail, but he didn't have a ship. He needed a large clipper ship for each voyage to be profitable. Or he needed one of the new ships he had heard about but not even seen. It is operated by a steam propeller as well as sails. A regular steamboat would not do because of the huge waves in the ocean. He would like to have a propeller-driven vessel.

He went to Señor Moreno with his idea.

Señor Moreno smiled and said, "If I can acquire such a ship, what would our financial arrangement be?"

"Señor Moreno, I propose that since you would be supplying the capital and your servant supplying the labor and sailing expertise, you take 55 percent of the profits, and I take 45 percent. In addition, you would be paid 5 percent of the gross value of the cargo for booking the ship."

Señor Moreno seemed surprised at John's generous proposition and accepted immediately. "I will do what is necessary," Señor Moreno said.

While John, Matt, and Mark were waiting for the ship to arrive from England via New York, the three of them worked on the Pensacola dock, loading the sailing ships with lumber and cotton.

When spring came, with Señor Moreno's permission, John took Maria out for long walks on the many lush tunnel-like paths through the thickets around Pensacola. They wandered by lazy-limbed live oaks covered with Spanish moss and wildflowers in their springtime radiance. He marveled at her beauty and told her of his love for her. They often lay on the pine-covered ground in secluded places. He would undress her to the waist, caress and kiss her olive skin, and gently rub her beneath her skirt until she cried out in ecstasy. She would then take him to her and bring him pleasure and release. But he never fully undressed himself or her because he did not feel the time for that had yet arrived. He loved her dearly, but he hesitated to take her youth. He was afraid that something might happen that would take him away. He did not want her ever to feel betrayed by him. She still had her virginity, and he had his past to worry about.

The ship finally arrived in the fall of 1858 when John had almost given up hope that it would ever come. The *Great Southern*, as she was called, was over two hundred feet long, painted red and black, with three masts and two smokestacks. The churning of the dual propellers was the feature that made it distinct. It docked at the Pensacola wharf and immediately drew a crowd of onlookers. Señor Moreno, having heard that it was coming into the harbor, was at the wharf to greet the crew and lined up on deck to impress those who were watching her dock.

John, Matt, and Mark came running down to the ship as Señor Moreno was boarding. He saluted the crew as John and the Hanshaws' caught up with him on deck. "Splendid," was all Señor Moreno could say as he inspected the ship. They all met the officers of the ship and departed to Señor Moreno's house to celebrate.

The following day, John was instructed in all the aspects of operating the vessel. John and the crew took it out for a cruise in the gulf, and John was pleased with how quickly he felt comfortable piloting it. It was a magnificent vessel!

The *Great Southern* turned out to be a profitable investment as she carried lumber and cotton to England, France, and up and down the East Coast between Boston and Baltimore. Sometimes John captained the ship; other times, he stayed home, and Matt or Mark took her out, usually together, with Matt serving as captain.

On one of Matt's cruises, his ship was stopped and boarded by a British ship. They were looking for someone, but neither Matt nor Mark could remember the name when they returned. They thought it might have been Gaygan. This made John wary. Why would they have stopped the *Great Southern* to look for him? He had to find out; otherwise, he could be in serious trouble.

CHAPTER 9

THE MILL TOWN: MILTON, FLORIDA

John and Maria, with Señor Moreno as chaperone, finally made a trip up the Blackwater to Milton. Milton was alive with activity. They saw a large wharf with several ships being loaded, a shipyard, a cotton warehouse, and the county courthouse; all situated reasonably near the river.

They arrived on a Saturday, just in time for a hanging on the courthouse square. A convicted murderer was climbing the steps of the gallows as they disembarked from their boat and walked up from the river. People had come from all over Santa Rosa County and beyond to witness the event. Many had spread picnic cloths on the ground. This was an exciting event. In fact, some had spent Friday night so they would not miss the execution. The officials asked the convicted man if he had any last words, but he was trembling so badly that he could not speak. They put a sack over his head, dropped a noose around his neck, and stood him over the trapdoor on the gallows. A man, obviously a preacher, said some words to the prisoner, and the trapdoor fell open. The condemned man fell and jerked for a moment, and then it was over. A cheer went up from the crowd.

Apparently, there was no sympathy for the executed man except perhaps from his family.

John, Maria, and Señor Moreno made their way through the crowd surrounding the courthouse, and two blocks from the river, they reached a residential area. John noticed a white two-story house with gables and green storm shutters. It had Ionic columns on the front, and a railing enclosed the front porch. Azaleas, camellias, and gardenias adorned the front yard, and the front porch was richly decorated with blooming potted flowers. Two tall date palms stood like sentinels on each side of the porch. John immediately yearned to live there, and when he expressed his admiration for it, Maria agreed that it was a beautiful house. He went on excitedly about how this would be the ideal place to live and harbor his ship nearby, and if he anchored the ship at Milton, he wouldn't have to be as concerned about hurricanes that threatened in the summer and fall. He would also be a few miles closer to the lumber sources and cotton on which his business depended. He ended by saying he would have to talk to the owner and try to acquire the house. Maria simply smiled happily by his side.

He knocked on the door, and a lady opened it. John was told that a gentleman was renting the house from the owner, a Mr. Ian McCaskill, who, at present, was living in Alabama. The trio then left for Pensacola.

While on a walk, John asked Maria if she would marry him if he were in a position to ask her. She did not understand the question. She asked, "What do you mean by in a position?" It was then that he told her about his past. She responded, "I will marry you regardless of what might happen. You are the only man I could ever love. I think I fell in love with you the first time I saw you in that horrible saloon." John smiled and kissed her tenderly.

John finally acquired the house after corresponding with Mr. McCaskill for several weeks. John's lawyer closed the deal on the property.

CHAPTER 10

MARIA SENT TO SPAIN

Señor Moreno knew that John's arrival in Pensacola was the best thing that ever happened to him. John was an astute businessman, honest, tireless, and always generous with Moreno sharing in the profits. He could not have a better business partner than John.

But he felt responsible for his late brother, Maria's father, Señor Don Carlos Moreno, to have Maria receive a proper Spanish Catholic education and to marry well into a Spanish family.

He could not muster the courage to discuss it with John without reason. Further, he could lecture Maria about it, but he could not voice his opinion to John because John had never asked for his permission to marry Maria because of his trouble with the British navy. The fact that John had not asked for Maria's hand also bothered Moreno. Not knowing all the facts gave Señor Moreno the impression that John did not intend to marry Maria.

Señor Moreno trusted John in business, but he did not know John's view on women and matters of the heart. So Moreno made his plans for Maria, and they did not include John, who was not Spanish or Catholic and had not asked permission to marry her. Those things brought Moreno to his decision.

So while John was at sea with the *Great Southern* in the summer of 1860, Maria sailed, unhappily, for Spain.

When John returned, he was surprised not to see Maria standing on the wharf waiting to embrace him.

"Where is Maria?" he asked nobody in particular.

Mark Hanshaw walked over to John and motioned for John to come to the end of the wharf to talk. "John, I don't know much about it, but Señor Moreno sent Maria away on a Spanish ship about three days after you left. The ship came the day after your departure. Maria's things were loaded on the ship, and it left early the following morning. Maria almost had to be carried aboard the ship. She obviously knew nothing about the trip. She was still in her bedclothes and robe and was forced to the ship by servants, one on each side," Mark told John.

John was angry for the first time Mark had known him. His face was bright red, and his hands shook. He took Mark's horse without asking and rode to Moreno's house. He barged into the house without slowing down for the maid and went looking for Moreno. Out of respect, he had always referred to him as Señor Moreno.

On this day, he shouted loudly, "Moreno! You son of a bitch. Where are you?"

"He is in Washington," one of the servants said.

"He won't be back for a long time," another servant added.

John started cooling down and considered some nonviolent form of revenge.

"Are you servants free?"

"No, suh."

"Does Moreno own you?"

"No, suh."

"Who does?" John continued his questions.

"We belong to the ship, 'lease that's what Marse Moreno says." Moreno had feathered his nest with slaves without telling John, whom he knew would disapprove.

He looked at corporate records of the *Great Southern* and noted an item under fixed assets that listed eight slaves by name, gender, year of birth, and cost:

Bought	Year	Birth Name	Amount
1858	1840	Cindy Lou	$900 110lbs
1858	1841	Bettye	$850 110lbs (sick when got)
1858	1835	Lawrence	$1,500 180lbs
1858	1836	Kenneth	$1,500 190lbs
		(Boy 10) Willie	
		(Boy 8*) Clyde	$1,000 for 4 children
		(Girl 8*) Belle	
		(Girl 9) Leah *Died	

"Cindy Lou, Bettye, Lawrence, and Kenneth!" John shouted. They each said "heah" when John called their names. "Where are the kids?" John inquired.

"Two died, and two sold off," Kenneth answered.

"Y'all wait, I got a surprise for you," John said.

In an hour, John was back with freedom certificates for the whole bunch, including the children. He appointed himself their guardian. This made John feel better, but he still wanted his Maria in his arms.

John knew Maria was in Spain, but he knew he could not find her without more information. Further, Señor Moreno stayed gone for over two years negotiating with the U.S. government to protect his cash in Northern banks and his securities from seizure. He bought three gunboats for the Union navy and gave the U.S. Army $10,000 to help finance a Florida cavalry unit. Further, he agreed to spy for the United States, which he did not plan to do. He also signed an oath of allegiance to the USA.

John wrote to Señor Moreno asking where he had sent Maria. Señor Moreno wrote him a long rambling letter telling why it was best for Maria to marry a Spanish Catholic from a good family.

Nevertheless, John kept the shipping company going. He sent Señor Moreno a new agreement that gave forty common stock shares of a total of one hundred to Señor Moreno and forty shares to himself, five shares each to Matt and Mark, and ten shares to the crew. Further, profits were to be divided based on stock ownership in addition to salaries. Señor Moreno signed and returned the papers without question. He knew he had no choice if he wanted to keep John as his captain and partner.

CHAPTER 11

JOHN'S WOULD-BE CAPTOR, OLIVER WATSON

In the fall of that same year, an Englishman came to Milton. He had heard that the *Great Southern* was there and wanted to question its owner. Little did John know that Señor Moreno had bought the ship in John's real name, which John had inadvertently signed when he struck a deal with Moreno. Soon, John heard that the Englishman was in town, and he prepared himself.

The Englishman came to John's house, and John invited him in. "I have been looking for you for a long time, John Geoghegan," the Englishman said as he withdrew a pistol from his coat and pointed it at John. "You must return with me to London to stand trial for murder."

"That is unlikely," John said.

Matt and Mark stood up from hiding places on opposite sides of the living room, Matt from behind a davenport and Mark from behind a wardrobe, each aiming shotguns at the Englishman.

"Drop your weapon," John said, and he complied. "We do not wish to harm you," John said to put the Englishman more at ease.

"You will eventually be apprehended. My associates know of your whereabouts," John's would-be captor responded defiantly.

"I'll worry about that later. Right now, we have to decide what to do with you," John replied. "What is your name?" John asked the Englishman.

"Oliver Watson, Royal British Navy," he answered.

John took on a serious demeanor. "I am not a murderer, at least not in the sense that I killed anyone with malice or for gain," John said firmly.

John spent at least two hours explaining the events and answering Oliver's questions. By that time, John had convinced Oliver of his innocence of the crimes he was charged with. Oliver said the ship they stopped was the *Viper,* a notorious slave ship, and he was certain it was not returning slaves to West Africa. That and John's explanation of the envelope containing $1,000, which John sent to the Royal Navy by Rodney Huffman, were convincing evidence of John's innocence.

"Do others really know my whereabouts?" asked John.

"No," Oliver responded. "I was merely trying to bluff you when I said that."

"If I set you free based on what you know, what will you do?"

"I don't know," replied Oliver honestly.

"Then stay with me, pretend you are still pursuing me, and I will show proof of my innocence," John suggested.

Oliver Watson knew he could never exonerate John in a court in England. After all, a member of the aristocracy had been killed.

"I have a better idea," Watson said. His last official report to England stated that John Geoghegan had died of yellow fever in 1855. He resigned from his position and signed on with John Smith.

Oliver Watson was a free spirit with no living family and nothing to tie him down, which was why he resigned from his position in England so readily. He was a delightful fellow to associate with after he was convinced of John's innocence.

CHAPTER 12

NORTHERN HOSTILITY: JOHN'S LACK OF KNOWLEDGE OF MORENO'S PLAN

As time slipped by, the rumors of war between the North and South increased. John found that the Northern ports were increasingly difficult to deal with. Sarcasm and outright hostility grew worse with each trip. John was interested in making money, so he didn't let attitude bother him.

John had been upset and restless since Señor Moreno had sent Maria to Spain without so much as a goodbye.

John knew that Señor Moreno sent Maria for proper education and to learn the Spanish culture since the opportunities in Spain were beyond the scope of the local Catholic school. But John was unaware of the arranged marriage that Moreno had already made sure took place.

CHAPTER 13

MICHAEL SMITH

Michael Smith, the son of Edward Smith, an Alabama planter, had spent his youth in Bagdad, Florida. Because his mother died of complications at Michael's birth, his paternal grandmother Margaret raised him. His father had neither the time nor the inclination to raise Michael on his plantation near Selma in the Black Belt. His father was ambitious and had acquired two thousand acres by the time he was thirty years of age. Margaret saw to it that Michael was well-educated. It was his father's profits from cotton and other crops that made it possible for him to attend Harvard and Oxford for advanced studies.

Michael was intelligent and just as ambitious as his father. He was also very taken with the English upper class and how they spoke. And so, he was determined to become proficient in the English language to the extent that nobody would even question that he was a member of the English gentry or nobility. Further, since his field of study was languages, he was fluent in French, Spanish, German, and Italian. He went so far as to research and found an English family of the nobility named Smythe, the last member of which died 150 years earlier. So he gave himself the title of Sir Michael of Smythebury.

Overtime, he was accepted by the English nobility. Being still a young man, he applied for and received an officer's commission in the Royal British Navy. His mentor Captain Nathan Woolsey trained him well and facilitated his rise to a commander in ten years. During those years, he met and became friends with John Geoghegan.

When the War Between the States became inevitable, Michael resigned from his commission and returned home. He visited the secretary of war of the United States as 'Sir Michael,' a British navy commander (retired), and offered his services. The secretary was completely taken in by Michael's demeanor. Michael was charged with moving around the South as a spy and filing reports on his observations of Confederate military activity. For his services, he received a generous salary and expense allowance. Michael then secretly contacted the military authorities of the Confederacy in Richmond. He advised the CSA secretary of war of his assignment and his dedication to the South. He received a letter from the secretary endorsing his activities as a double agent. The Confederacy provided only an expense account.

Michael, sagacious by nature, filed reports that sounded useful to the Union but, in the end, were not for various reasons. The courier was late because Michael would have him delayed by rebel blockades; the courier's directions, allegedly prepared by another spy, would send him to the wrong Union command post. Michael was creative in providing useless information. Occasionally, Michael sent useful and timely reports. But he would alert the Confederate troops involved so they could be prepared and subtly respond in a manner that would not expose Michael. He would disclose the locations and sacrifice CSA's unguarded "contraband" from time to time so he would not lose his credibility.

He moved from Richmond to New Orleans and other seaport cities, enjoying his expense accounts posing as an English newspaper reporter.

He had visited the Pensacola area early in the war and located John Geoghegan in Milton. They talked most of an early winter night in 1861. As a result of their discussions, Michael presented his credentials to the Union army at Fort Pickens and was allowed to use the fort as a convenient base of operation. The Union ships arriving and departing provided a wealth of information Michael furnished to the Confederacy as a double agent. The Union was pleased with his work, and the rebels were elated to have the intelligence Michael provided. The Union provided a small, fast ship to slip him into Southern coastal cities. Michael somehow usually managed to be in Fort Pickens when John sailed. Michael Smith was indispensable to John in running the Union blockade at Pensacola.

CHAPTER 14

SUSANNA

Señor Moreno finally returned just before the war. He expected Cindy Lou, Bettye, Lawrence, and Kenneth to be at the wharf to greet him. Some of his children, grandchildren, nephews, and nieces were there, but none of his house slaves were present. Señor Moreno did not know that John had them hidden in the pine forest a few miles up the Blackwater River, awaiting the *Great Southern*'s next departure.

Señor Moreno was accompanied on his Washington trip by his assistant and lover, a lovely light-skinned Negress named Susanna, known among a privileged few as Saber, a nickname abbreviated from the saber-toothed tiger. She acquired that nickname from a primitive Baptist preacher who sexually excited Susanna, especially when she heard him preach. The more graphic he was in describing the decadence, which always led to the periodic demise of Israel, the more aroused she got. Nobody knew when it started, but Brother John Bob Andrews could see Susanna in the segregated balcony's front row with her hand underneath her skirt from the pulpit. Susanna kept the church utility shed behind the church, ready to meet after the service. Susanna was a loud fornicator.

One night, while the deacons were meeting in the little church, they suddenly heard Susanna's loud groan. They followed the noise to the shed. A lantern in the shed revealed Susanna and the pastor without any clothes except socks. Brother John Bob shouted, "She is like a saber-toothed tigress who came to devour me! She is of the devil! She has had me in a trance for weeks!"

Susanna ran home naked while John Bob continued to blame Susanna and Satan for the whole chain of events. He cast himself as a victim. But his excuse did not convince. John Bob was dismissed, and the deacons vowed silence regarding the matter. So the story about Saber must have come from Susanna herself.

Señor Moreno was pleased with Susanna in spite of her legendary sex drive or perhaps because of it. She could act refined when called upon to do so. Moreno had freed her and acted as her guardian. She was light enough that Moreno presented her as of Spanish and Egyptian lineage when they traveled.

CHAPTER 15

MORENO APOLOGIZES

When Moreno and Susanna went home, and none of his slaves were either at the wharf or there, he grew furious. But, he had told John that the shipping company would use no slaves. So he had broken his word. Therefore, he had nothing to be angry about. Further, all the time he spent away from the shipping company while in Washington was to protect his personal assets, not the company assets. Yet John saw to it that he got a paycheck and his share of any bonuses paid. John was fair to him and had never gone back on his word. And now that it had been revealed why John had not asked for Maria's hand in marriage, he saw how wrong he had been. John was probably the most honorable man he had ever known. He deceived John, something John would never have done to him. And he had sent Maria to marry a man she did not love when she had loved John for years. In fact, she had told him that she believed she had fallen in love with him the first time she saw him.

He considered what he could do to correct his mistakes. The first thing to do was to apologize to John and help him unite with Maria, to hell with race and religious differences. Maria and John were both Christians. The Catholics were no more Christians than the Anglicans and Episcopalians. Faith in Jesus was the basis of the three. How much difference was there between the churches?

Señor Moreno would talk to John, apologize to him, and tell him where Maria was. And then he would say to him the worst part.

Señor Moreno was honest and, to a point, candid. He told John that Maria went to a convent in Ronda, near Malaga, and was studying there. He also told John that Maria had learned much over the last two years. He gave John the address of the convent.

Señor Moreno could carry the story no further.

CHAPTER 16

THE FIRST BLOCKADE RUN: THE UNION BOARDS THE CAROLINA

When John again sailed commercially, it was under very different circumstances. He flew the American flag, but since the war had started, the Yankees at Fort Pickens sent Boston Whalers out to board his vessel. He easily maneuvered past them into the open gulf. They were infuriated and fired at the *Great Southern* to show their indignation. The Northern blockade was not yet entirely in place, so John got out safely. He knew then that he must change his tactics, or he would not survive the war.

As attrition had depleted the original crew of the *Great Southern*, John replaced them with Michel, Juan, and Ricardo, his first three acquaintances in Pensacola. He had also hired a couple of their friends. So his crew was already predominantly Spanish. Observing this fact, John came up with his "cover" when running the blockades. He would find other work in his company for his English crew members and replace them with Spaniards. Then he would sail under Mexican colors.

He charted a course for Veracruz, the destination of his nonmilitary cargo. When the *Great Southern* arrived at Veracruz, John decided what he would do. First, with permission of the owners, he investigated those subtle differences that would convey the authenticity of his ship's origin. The crosses in miniature and the similar Christian statues were examples of what John was looking for. Mexican blankets were another. He bought some of these and other items in case the crew didn't have their own. John bought a set of used canvas sails and extra secondhand canvas. He also procured all the black paint the vendor had because he figured he would need it sooner or later. He then purchased one hundred gallons of white paint. Finally, he bought traditional peasant wear for the crew. John had his crew paint the ship black except for the top four feet of the sides and stern. The upper four feet they painted white. He changed the ship's name from *Great Southern* to *Carolina* and returned to Pensacola.

John, the crew, and the *Carolina* were saved from Union blockaders and other Union gunboats on several occasions by their Mexican disguise. The *Carolina* had never been boarded by the Union vessels it encountered. She had been stopped a few times, and the crew had faked cooperation by immediately stopping when requested to do so. The language difference between English and Spanish seemed to create a psychological barrier and subconscious acceptance of the Mexican facade. Finally, the day came when an overly zealous Union captain requested permission to board. He and his officers were shown official-looking paperwork in English and Spanish to validate their voyage. Then they were taken below to inspect the bales of cotton marked "Producto de Mexico." Under the cotton, lumber was concealed. Since the *Carolina* was only 150 miles south of Pensacola, the Union captain, Captain Thetford, drew a map of the Gulf Coast showing how far off course the *Carolina* was and added a large question mark. Michel drew a direct line to Havana from Veracruz. Besides that line, he drew three Confederate flags, indicating three Confederate raiders. He then drew a dot representing the *Carolina* going northwest toward Bagdad, Mexico, not to pick up Texas cotton but to avoid Confederate raiders who followed them for several days and nights before giving up. Michel skillfully drew symbols representing Confederate ships in pursuit. In short, Michel made the Union officers believe their story. The Union officers thanked Captain Michel and departed.

Captain Thetford's and Michel's map:

CHAPTER 17

HALLOWEEN: THIRTEENTH BLOCKADE RUN

John's early blockade runs were perfectly successful. The Union military had written Pensacola off as a place to run the blockade. So the army and navy considered a Pensacola assignment to be a safe one. The safety did not lessen the discomfort of the heat and insects, however. But the safe and laid-back Union attitude did work to the advantage of the *Carolina* and her crew. The first twelve runs and returns all went well, except for the aforementioned Union inspection encounter. The *Carolina* was never detected at Pensacola. There were several close calls because ships unexpectedly left the Pensacola docks. But the Union's overconfidence helped to keep the *Carolina* safe.

On John's thirteenth blockade-run attempt, things didn't go well. First, there was no light signal from Fort Pickens. John decided to proceed anyway. Since Pensacola was used for R & R by the Union blockaders, there was always the possibility of encountering a Union vessel in Pensacola Bay. On this night, when his signaler was down with influenza, so sick that he could not stand, John saw a Union ship entering the bay as he was exiting. Further, on this night, an electrical storm came in from the southwest after John had committed to proceed. The resulting lightning created flashes rivaling daylight that lasted several seconds and occurred continuously. The *Carolina* was sighted at about the same time by the Union ship entering the bay and by the soldiers on guard duty at Fort Pickens.

It happened to be All Saints' Eve, known as Halloween (from Hallowed Eve) by immigrants who introduced it to America quite recently. Starting in the 1840s, its popularity was spreading, so for Halloween, the soldiers at Fort Pickens had been entertained earlier in the evening by a speaker who claimed to be the bastard son of Edgar Allen Poe from Salem, Massachusetts. With a woeful demeanor, the gentleman read works of Poe and told terrifying tales of headless horsemen, witches, zombies, and ghost ships manned by rotting corpses and skeletons roaming the seas. This set a macabre mood enhanced by the stormy evening. Consequently, when the unlighted *Carolina* was revealed by the lightning, the Yankees at Fort Pickens were mesmerized by a dark ship in the bay's pass. In the two or three minutes it took the Union soldiers at Fort Pickens to return from awe to reality and think, "Blockade runner," John had started his steam engines and gone to full speed ahead. The *Carolina* quickly passed the unexpected Union vessel, perhaps one hundred yards to the *Carolina's* port side.

The storm had passed over and lost strength after landfall. The lightning had dissipated as well. The Union blockader fired blindly at the *Carolina* as it turned hard to port. Their volley fell harmlessly into the whitecaps of the gulf. John and the crew of the *Carolina* felt the unwelcome scraping of sand beneath them. John had lost his usually precise knowledge of the *Carolina's* position because of the distractions. When the lightning flashed again, his view and the compass indicated he was too far to starboard and out of the channel. He made the necessary course corrections as the Union blockader was closing in on him. He felt the sand again and prayed. The grabbing of the sand and the propellers' momentary stopping were frightening. As he pondered what to do, John saw the Union vessel run aground in even more shallow water behind him. Fort Pickens cannons were fired aimlessly in the *Carolina's* direction.

John quickly cut the engine and called, "All hands on deck. Who will, for a two-hundred-dollar bonus, volunteer to take the lifeboats and go capture and destroy that Union blockader?"

"Si!" All hands went up.

"You will be left behind and have to make your way back to safety either by stealing the Union ship or making it back by land through Union-held territory."

"Si!" the crew repeated.

"You can't all go, and some I must have." John selected ten men, some of who were just hitching a ride to Havana, appointed the leader, and issued them weapons. They then departed. The decrease of approximately one ton of weight on the ship made it easier to get back into the channel and proceed toward Havana.

Before the *Carolina* was over the horizon, John saw a small point of light that appeared to be a firelight from a burning ship. This gave John hope that his volunteers were doing what they had set out to do.

CHAPTER 18

DESTROYING UNION FRIGATES

John was fed up with the damn Yankees after the close call on Halloween night. He had reached the breaking point. Further, in spite of Senor Moreno's explanation and apology, John still held resentment for his loss of Maria and the way Moreno handled it. And he sensed that Moreno was holding something back and keeping an urgent backlog of contracts for John to fulfill before going to Spain. John took Moreno at face value and tried to believe him. Moreno was afraid of what John might do if he was aware of the arranged wedding.

John was filled with pent-up anger, which had grown over time. He wanted to take that anger out on the bastards who were blocking his port. So one night, when the moon was bright, carrying cannons instead of cargo and with a ragtag bunch of retired military sailors instead of his Spaniards, he sped past Fort Pickens with the Union guards and artillerymen sleeping, or distracted and into open water a mile from the shore.

In preparation for the occasion, he had made the bow of the *Carolina* a battering ram capable of piercing a wooden ship below the water line. The USS *Bedford* and the USS *Dorsett*, two Union frigates, were patrolling in the Gulf of Mexico off Pensacola. They were heavily armed gunboats equipped to prevent any attempt to run the blockade.

When John was a mile out in the gulf, he turned the *Carolina* back to face the shore. He was aware that the two frigates were rapidly advancing toward the *Carolina*, so he began to sail back toward the one on the port side. He knew that a head-on collision would be fatal to the Union ship.

He gave the order. "Full ahead to impact the Union vessel to port."

Matt was at the wheel for this special event. "Aye, aye, Captain."

When the *Carolina* was about fifty yards away, John said, "Half speed and at twenty yards, idle engines, prepare for bow impact."

Matt did a perfect job. Using the rudder only, he burst the bow of the *Dorsett*.

"Full back, excellent, Mr. Hanshaw." Water was pouring into the bow of the USS *Dorsett*.

"Thank you, Captain Smith, sir," Matt answered.

"Quarter speed, heading due south," John ordered.

When Matt had the *Carolina* headed south, John gave the order. "Full ahead."

The USS *Bedford* had been farther away when the *Carolina* first appeared. When it reached the *Dorsett*, it had to rescue the crew of the *Dorsett*. Her stern was already beginning to rise. Union sailors were climbing from the *Dorsett* to the *Bedford*, which had come alongside.

While all the crew of the *Bedford* was engaged in rescue efforts, John had Matt bring the *Carolina* back within effective cannon range. Rather than take the lives of many Union sailors, John had the cannoneers shoot the stack and the masts off the *Bedford*. Finally, they blasted the propellers to immobilize the rescue vessel. The *Carolina* had maintained a position from which they were never a target for the *Bedford* cannons. After sufficiently embarrassing the blockaders, they went to Havana to purchase a load of whatever they could sell to the Confederacy.

CHAPTER 19

JOHN FINDS MARIA

As soon as the opportunity arose, John sailed to Europe to find Maria. After a rough Atlantic crossing, the *Carolina* reached the French port of La Havre to trade with the French merchants. John then left La Havre and sailed down the English Channel and around the Iberian Peninsula through the Straits of Gibraltar and east to Malaga. After the *Carolina* was safely anchored in the harbor at Malaga, John instructed the crew to alternate between ship duty and shore leave. John left Matt and Mark in charge of the ship and took Oliver with him to find horses to rent or purchase for the trip to Ronda. After haggling for too long, John and Oliver purchased two healthy-looking horses for a reasonable price. John and Oliver then made the long ride up to Ronda.

White adobe houses decorated with flowers in the windows often appeared on the way. They would occasionally stop and converse with the local farmers and herdsmen. The locals were quick to warn them of bandits operating in the area. They spoke of robberies, kidnapping, and even one fatal shooting of a foreigner, either an American or an Englishman. This was disturbing to John and Oliver.

Nevertheless, they were well armed, and now they knew they must be very cautious and stay alert for possible ambush sites. They made it to Ronda and found the convent. John banged the metal knocker on the door, and after a few moments, a nun came to the entrance. She smiled and invited them into a lovely courtyard covered with flowers with two sycamore trees for shade. It would be a lovely place for meditation and prayer, John thought.

"How beautiful," John exclaimed.

"God's earth is a beautiful place," the nun replied. "And we try to gather as much beauty here as possible."

John was surprised at her English. It was English with an Irish accent.

"It appears you are God's work transplanted here from Ireland."

"Aye," she said as she blushed and smiled. "Thank you, kind stranger."

"John Smith, and this is Oliver Watson," John responded quickly.

"And I am Sister Mary. How may I help you?"

"We are looking for Maria Moreno. We are old friends of hers." Sister Mary frowned. "Maria was here, and she was a wonderful young lady. But a while back, she was married to a Spanish gentleman in an arranged marriage," Sister Mary explained. "Her husband, Señor Lopez, was recently kidnapped by bandits and is being held for ransom."

John immediately felt weak and turned pale. He had to sit down on a nearby bench.

"Where may we find Señora Lopez?" Oliver asked.

"She lives three streets north in a *casa grande*. You will easily recognize it. Lopez is spelled out in the tile at the entrance," Sister Mary elaborated.

"Could my friend and I have a cool drink of water?" Oliver asked. "Of course," came the reply.

After John had recovered from the revelation of Maria's marriage, they thanked Sister Mary and walked toward the Lopez house. When they reached the gate, Oliver discreetly stopped and allowed John to walk up the brick-paved path and the steps to the front door alone. John had said nothing on the walk from the convent, and Oliver could only imagine his anguish.

John stood upright and straight and knocked on the door. A young servant girl asked in Spanish, "Who may I say is calling?"

John replied, "John Smith."

The young girl said, "Uno momento," and went to get Maria. After a few moments, Maria opened the door, trembling. She pulled John inside and closed the door. She then wrapped herself around him and began to sob with joy and regret. John embraced her, and neither spoke a word for several minutes. Maria was wearing a puffy white blouse scooped low and worn off the shoulder with a long full, colorful yellow skirt. After a few minutes, they held each other loosely and just looked at one another pensively. Neither of them could think of what to say.

John finally spoke. "I have thought of you many times every single day since you disappeared from my world."

"And I also," Maria replied. "Uncle Francisco is a good man, and he thought he was doing what was best for me." Maria continued. "I have learned much and have a wider world opened to me, but I would gladly have sacrificed all of it to have stayed with you." She led him to a chair and sat close in a chair, facing him.

"God, you are still so beautiful," John whispered.

She smiled and said, "So are you." Then, Maria resumed her story. "My uncle never realized the depth of our feelings for each other, and I think he had some doubts regarding your intentions toward me. I tried to make him understand, but it was no use in the end. I would have disgraced my uncle and myself if I had not abided by his wishes. So my uncle made arrangements, and I sailed tearfully away on a Spanish ship while you were at sea. My uncle also wanted me to marry well. But the wealthy landowner he had corresponded with and received good reports about through correspondence with local officials and clergy left one thing out of his résumé. He was seventy-nine years old. Further, because of his power and benevolence in the community, no one would dare mention this when corresponding with Uncle Francisco. He is a good man and a gentleman. And I love him as a friend. We attend Mass and social events together, but I made it clear to him from the beginning that we would never consummate our marriage. He was satisfied with that because he told me he was in the terminal stage of syphilis and would not live much longer. In fact, he may already be dead. He was kidnapped by bandits two days ago in his carriage on the way to Malaga. He is getting frail, and I am afraid he won't live long in captivity, even if he is alive. The bandits sent Emmanuel, my husband's driver, back with a ransom note asking for a ridiculously large amount of money, more than twice Señor Lopez's assets. They said they would kill him on Friday if they did not receive payment by then, and today is Tuesday."

PART III

CHAPTER 20

BEN JERNIGAN, JACOB RUCKER, AMANDA RUCKER

"Even my damn skiff boat!" Jacob Rucker had begun to talk to himself out loud in the last few weeks, snarling through clenched teeth. He sat in a ladder-back chair, looking out at the darkness through an upstairs window of his house, two blocks from the Blackwater River. Upstairs, the house was a little warmer. The second-floor windows had not been broken by the secessionists.

With his white beard covered in several quilts, Jacob looked much older than his fifty-five years.

"Were they afraid the Union would turn it into a damn gunboat?" The only light he had came from a single candle stuck to the windowsill with wax, and its flickering light danced on the walls. He coughed intermittently, using the corners of the quilt like a handkerchief.

Those bastard, ignorant, fool secessionists. Those Yankees gonna kick our asses. What are we gonna do, throw cotton balls? Beard is supposed to be on our side. He looked like he enjoyed destroying what it took 50 years to build. I hope he burns in hell. "Scorched earth, my ass. Lunacy was what it was. I'd like to set him on fire as he did on Milton! They afraid of them sissies from up North." He coughed a productive cough and pulled the quilts to his mouth.

Amanda, Jacob's daughter, climbed the steep steps to the two-room upstairs, carefully holding a bowl in one hand and the stair rail with the other.

"I made some chowder with the bream Zeke brought. It should do us for a couple of days," she said, trying to convey optimism.

Jacob looked to his right from where her voice came. He wondered how she made her way to him without more light.

"Thanks," he said to her dark form, moving toward him.

As Jacob took the bowl from Amanda, the quilts fell from his shoulders. He clumsily pulled the quilts back in place with his right hand while holding the chowder bowl with the other hand, balancing it on his knee. The chowder briefly quieted the cough.

"Has anyone else left town?" Jacob asked.

"No, Daddy, not that I know of. Zeke would have mentioned it, I'm sure," Amanda replied.

"There ain't many folks left. Fine with me. They all knew where I stood on this whole damn mess. So they helped Colonel Beard finish me off. What we got left?" Jacob asked.

"Not much, Daddy. But we'll get through this."

"Before they ran off up to Alabama, they broke up everything in the house that they didn't steal. If I hadn't been down with the fever, I might coulda stopped 'em," Jacob said.

"If you hadn't been down sick, you'd got yourself killed," Amanda said. "When this cold snap passes, things will be better." Amanda was still trying to sound optimistic.

"Get Zeke to board up the windows and find some doors to replace the ones that mob broke up. Zeke may be a slave, but he's got more sense than all them chicken shit rebel bastards combined," Jacob said. "I'm glad he came to work for us rather than take off to Mexico with other freed slaves. Zeke knew who to make as his guardian when they passed that stupid law ordering freed slaves to have guardians."

"I'm puttin' in a garden on Good Friday," Amanda said. She had a deep, pleasing voice that complemented her physical beauty. She carried herself in a regal fashion. Her elegant well-formed face and blond hair went well with her petite shapely figure. Jacob reckoned that they would have suffered more secessionist abuse if she had not arrived during their visit. Her captivating appearance tempered the men's enthusiasm for mayhem. When she arrived, the vandalism subsided, and the mob moved on, looking for other Unionists to harass.

"That's good, darlin'," Jacob replied. The cough still hadn't returned.

"Zeke hid his skiff before the Confederates got here and burned everything. So it looks like we gonna be eatin' nothin' but fish for a while," Amanda said. "I'll be back in a minute."

She walked back to the stairs and felt her way down. She came back with her father's whiskey and the lamp she left burning at the foot of the stairs earlier.

"How you feelin', Daddy?" she asked. When she was midsentence, his coughing started again. She moved the bowl that had been resting on his lap. Then she picked up his whiskey bottle beside the chair and held it for him to take a long swig. She saw that he was growing weaker.

"Help me over to the bed, Mandy." She reached around him and his quilts, and with her left arm around his back, she guided him to the bed on the other side of the small room. After she helped him lie down, she pulled the ladder-back chair to his bedside and sat down by him. She set the lamp on a bedside table.

"Mandy, please get me some more cover. I got a bad chill." Mandy loaded him down with three quilts.

"Thank God your fever broke and you got well," Jacob said. "There ain't no more work for a shipwright around here. So I might as well go on to be with Mama. If it wasn't for worrying about my sweet Mandy . . ." Tears filled his eyes.

"Daddy, don't worry. You gonna get well, and with Zeke's help, we'll make it."

"Mandy, if I don't get well, you get Zeke to find Ben. He'll help you get to a safe place. I love you, Mandy."

Amanda kissed her father on the forehead. "I love you too, Daddy." She took the lamp and walked to her bed in the adjoining upstairs room. The whiskey helped the cough and let Jacob sleep.

Amanda tried to sleep but could not settle her mind for sleep. She thought, *Thank God Mama didn't live to see all this.* Their shipyard had been burned. She remembered Colonel Beard's Confederate troops burning everything they thought the Yanks could use, even Daddy's fishing boat. She recalled several Confederate enlisted men attacking her daddy with rifle butts when he tried to intervene, knocking him unconscious. He already had influenza when that happened. She thought about how he had changed since then. He was bitter and agitated most of the time now. And he had taken to cussin'. Something he never did before. Though he was a deacon in the First Baptist Church, his drinking had gotten bad, and he talked to himself.

Finally, she got up, slipped into the other bedroom, and retrieved the whiskey. She drank an amount she deemed adequate for sleep but not enough for a hangover. She liked the warm feeling she got as the whiskey took hold. The sleep remedy worked quickly. Her last painful thoughts were of the poor widow with only a few bales of cotton on a wagon. She pleaded with Colonel Beard to allow her to take it back to Alabama. He refused and burned it.

Amanda wondered as she lay there how a man in Richmond, who may have never laid eyes on Milton or Pensacola, could make a decision that affected so many lives. Would he have done the same if it had been his ancestral home? *No,* she thought. He would somehow have found troops from somewhere else, or he would have taken Fort Pickens by continued bombardment until it was rubble, if necessary, so that he could protect his own.

Amanda Rucker, an educated lady, had memorized what Florida governor Richard Keith Call had said in January 1861 when he heard of the Florida secession votes: "You have opened the gates of hell, from which shall flow the curses of the damned to sink you to perdition." She admired the language but hated the message. He was right.

Jacob died the next day.

CHAPTER 21

BEN JERNIGAN: WAITING OUT THE WAR

Ben sat in his skiff off the mouth of Yellow River, where it empties into Blackwater Bay. The sun hinted at its debut as the blackness turned to gray. A soft breeze chilled the late December morning, causing his boat to gently rock and brush against the sawgrass. Behind him, porpoises chased mullet up Blackwater Bay, their dorsal fins playing peek-a-boo as they surged above and slid beneath the surface. Ben had three cane fishing poles prepared and extended over the side of the skiff.

He held one pole and had two mounted over the gunwales under the boat's seat. Redfish had been running for the last couple of days. The previous evening, he had floated down the river from his cabin in the Yellow River swamp. He had anchored off the river's mouth, eaten his supper of hard bread and honey, and then slept uncomfortably in his boat. He awoke before daylight. Fishing had become a significant part of his livelihood for the last few months. He used trot lines for catfish, a cast net mainly for mullet, and his cane pole for whatever was biting. He went about his new occupation, always watchful of discovery by Confederate cavalry units, which wandered down from Alabama like wolves hungry for flesh. They would either attempt to conscript him into the army, kill him, or imprison him as a Union sympathizer.

As Ben fished, the cork on his fishing line danced in time with each passing wave. He watched the cork and let his mind wander back to March '62, the previous year. He was on his way back from Arcadia on his fractious gray mule. As he gained high ground east of Pond Creek, he met up with an old freed slave from Milton. He knew the man only by his nickname "Snowball." The ancient white-bearded blue-black man approached him.

Without so much as a greeting, Snowball jabbed the air with his forefinger in the direction of the town and said, "Marse Ben, they say General Bragg pulled his troops out of Pensacola, and they's burnin' everything 'round here." Ben then saw the distant smoke, its blackness surging upward, defiling the blue sky. Ben felt limp and sick. He knew his boatyard was in ruin. And he hated the sons of bitches who burned it!

He didn't give a damn about the war. His contempt for the Union army equaled his feelings about secessionists. Since the Confederates pulled out, the hardship inflicted on him, and his people by scavengers on both sides was contemptible. They had been relatively happy, some even prosperous, before the war.

Ben was interrupted from his musing by a sudden forceful snatch on his line. He skillfully landed a sizable redfish, removed the hook from its mouth, and then dropped the fish in the skiff's well. By the time he baited his hook with cut bait and put his cane pole back over the side of the boat, he was once again lost in thought.

If he could keep himself stocked with meal, salt, lard, and preserved fruits and vegetables by bartering with his smoked fish and honey, he'd make it through another winter. Beekeeping, which had been an avocation before the war, contributed to his survival now. He damn sure wasn't going to fight. He never wanted secession in the first place. He knew slavery was on the way out, and like most people, he didn't own any slaves. Hell, he never even rented one to help build the small boats he sold for a living before the war.

Ben was one of the few people who decided to stay put now that the interior of West Florida had become a no-man's-land when the Confederates pulled out. The Union now held Pensacola and threatened the hinterland. The Confederate withdrawal left residents of Pensacola and Milton feeling as exposed as a salamander under a rock that had been suddenly lifted. Most everyone had bolted for the relative safety of South Alabama. The untrodden dirt streets of Milton were knee-deep in goldenrod and sand spurs. The windows of the homes and the few remaining stores were boarded up. The souls who remained there were like phantoms venturing out only when absolutely necessary.

Looking out across the bay, Ben saw that the sun was just beginning to glisten on the waves, now kicked up by a stiff north wind. A multitude of seagulls faced the wind, standing at attention on the countless cut timbers strewn along the shore. A few of the lumber, some of the smaller ones, were piled up like pickup sticks. But most of the logs were lined up horizontally in almost uniform rows, reminiscent of strips of corduroy. Many still floated in the bay. The timber was a reminder of what had been. These were giant yellow pines taken from the seemingly endless forest that reached from the Gulf Coast well up into South Alabama. The lumber he saw was cut before the mills burned, and now the Yankees were salvaging it for their purposes at Fort Pickens, which guarded the entrance to Pensacola Bay.

The massive virgin yellow pines that Ben recalled from earlier times had begun to recede inland. They were victims of wealthy men who sent slaves and immigrants to fell and drag them with axes, saws, chains, and oxen. Their torsos were floated down the ample watercourses to Blackwater sawmills to be transmuted into lumber, sashes, panel doors, venetian blinds, and ships. He missed hearing the mournful sound the wind made when it passed through the primeval forest giants. The war had stopped the cutting for a while. But he knew the virgins would be gone in another fifty years.

He had a good catch, so he started the arduous journey back up the river. He didn't want to be picked up through the field glass of some rebel or Union patrol. The swamp was his home now. He had retreated there to avoid conscription or worse fates. He had built a small log cabin concealed by a thick canebrake near the confluence of a creek and the river a short distance from the bay. He kept his beehives on a secluded hammock about a mile up Yellow River.

By the time Ben returned to his cabin about midmorning, he was exhausted from the trip upriver against the current. A lesser man might not have made it. After cleaning his fish and washing up, he entered his serviceable one-room dwelling. Burlap served as drapes over the two windows, one on each side of the cabin. Furnishing consisted of a narrow bed on the right side against the wall, a small table, two ladder-back chairs, a kerosene lamp, and a black iron pot hanging from a curved rod by the fireplace on the back wall. The fire he had built the previous evening was cold, and he couldn't start another one this time of day for fear of detection. He took off all his clothes, as was his custom, got in his primitive bed, and pulled the covers up over his head to get warm. He was asleep within minutes.

He dreamed of Ireland. He could move his arms up and down and fly in his dream, slowly moving over the sheep grazing in the green pasture below. A pretty red-haired child sitting on a wall looked up at him longingly. She was calling his name and pleading that he come down. He noticed that her mannerisms reminded him of Amanda.

Ben was a highly intelligent man. He read newspapers where they were available and listened to people who were knowledgeable about what had happened in the fragmented government of the States. He formed his opinion regarding the complex question as to why a war was believed necessary by Lincoln. The truth was a war was not required until the North invaded the South and the South rose to defend its homeland.

With his inconsistent words and behavior, Ben believed Lincoln was more interested in unconstitutionally keeping the southern states in the Union than in freeing the slaves.

Ben spent time alone in his cabin, thinking about why things turned out the way they had. He disliked Lincoln. The President of the United States was wrong to force the Southern States, who voluntarily joined the Union, to remain in the union if they chose to withdraw. Further, in addition to the unconstitutional prohibition to secede, the Constitution calls for the people to change the government if it becomes oppressive. The South was being oppressed by having to pay tariffs of 40 percent to the U.S. Treasury on the goods it purchased. Some said it comprised the revenue of the Federal Government, perhaps 70-80 percent.

The Southerners were primarily engaged in agriculture and forestry. Their significant products were cotton, tobacco, lumber, and to some extent, other products.

But Ben thought the South inherited the institution of slavery from their ancestors. Many Southerners did not like it, and it took jobs away from white men. But many saw nothing morally wrong with it based on the Bible and the Torah. That was generally how things were in the mid-1800s across the South.

Ben knew that estimates of what percent of Southerners owned slaves varied, and the number of slaves varied significantly among and within the states. In some places, twenty to twenty-five percent might be a reasonable estimate. In other areas, those estimates include slave owners who had only one to five slaves, representing probably fifty percent of slave owners, Ben reasoned.

As Ben lay in his bed, he ruminated. There were numerous anti-slavery societies in the South, perhaps 90 or more. They were led by Southern Christian evangelists. These progressive preachers were not in the mainstream of Southern Christian thinking. The majority of the Southerners left unquestioned the Christian Bible and the Jewish Torah. Both books accepted slavery as a seemingly benign institution of society.

Ben knew that people were wrong about some things. White people of the North and South believed blacks were inferior to whites. That included Abraham Lincoln, Jefferson Davis, and Robert E. Lee. Further, nobody wanted to mix with them except to the extent required by practical necessity. Occasionally, an owner or other white man, given the opportunity, would have voluntary or involuntary sexual intercourse with a slave.

Ben was hopeful regarding freedom for the slaves. Davis and Lee, who had freed their slaves, believed that the Africans, by exposure to civilization and Christianity, would eventually be ready to increase levels of freedom and avoid violence like what occurred in Haiti.

Many Southerners feared what would happen if the approximately four million slaves in the south were free. There was a slave uprising in Haiti from 1791 to 1804. Rioting slaves raped, mutilated, and murdered French Colonists. Finally, there were no whites left on the island. Ben shuttered, thinking about that.

The Southern leaders knew they had a severe problem because they inherited the practice of slavery. They envisioned a gradual, none-violent approach to emancipation, perhaps paying the slave owners for their loss with the money that used to be paid for tariffs. But the abolitionists of the North (Home of 18-hour factory work days and child labor) called for immediate slave uprisings and violence to accomplish emancipation.

Ben thought about Lincoln again. Lincoln could not or would not see the difficult position the South was in. He initially professed his adherence to States' Rights, preventing him from taking action. Ben believed Lincoln favored the North, which was more industrialized, and many deemed he favored their owners and executives. His real belief, apparently, was to have a strong central government with states being subdivisions thereof with limited powers. Though unconstitutional at the time, he took the country down that path. Lincoln never acknowledged the Southern secession as anything more than an internal rebellion within the United States of America. Some claimed that Lincoln was influenced by the fact that Northern industrialists wanted the South subdued by whatever means possible so that they could cheaply acquire the resources of the South.

So, Lincoln wanted war. The freeing of the slaves was the stated noble reason to invade the South. A victory would make Lincoln a hero. The Southern government sent peace negotiators to meet with Lincoln. However, Lincoln would not even talk with them even though they waited a month in Washington. Lincoln wanted a war that he mistakenly believed would be over quickly.

Lincoln knew the war was the only way to keep the southern states from leaving the Union. He knew that without the South, the North could not survive economically. A financial collapse would ruin the North unless it has its "Cash Cow." But to free the slaves seemed much more noble.

Ben was tired of working to survive and of thinking about some of the fools God put on this earth. He fell asleep.

CHAPTER 22

CALEB

As the half-light of evening fell over the swamp, Ben woke to a noise, a rustling of bushes outside the cabin. He pushed his blond hair out of his eyes and grabbed his knife from under his pillow. Without bothering to dress, he slipped quietly to the window facing the creek. He saw what looked like a Confederate butternut coat through the cattails along the creek. Though it was cold and Ben was naked, he climbed out the opposite window and crouched near the front of the opposite side of the cabin to wait. The butternut form moved closer, approaching the cabin door. When the intruder started to lift the latch, Ben lunged, pinning him to the small porch.

It was then that he realized it was a black man. Ben put his knife to his throat, trying to decide what to do.

The black man surprised him by saying, "Marse Ben, it's me, Caleb!"

Ben immediately stood up and helped the black man to his feet. Caleb was shaken and couldn't think what to say, especially with Ben standing there naked.

"That thing gonna shrivel up and go away ifin' you do't git some clothes on."

"Come inside," Ben said.

He then quickly put on his long underwear and, sitting on the bed, pulled on his socks. "Caleb, I'm gonna build a fire. It's late enough now. And while I'm doing that, please tell me what you're doing here."

Caleb looked nervously out at the swamp as he helped Ben with the fire. "Marse Ben, I'm sorry I slipped up like that. I wasn't sure this was your place. I been in these swamps for two days. You got anything to eat?"

Ben patiently replied yes, and as soon as the fire began to crackle, he set about to feed the runaway. "When you gonna tell me what you doin' here?"

"Marse Ben, Marse William Clayton sent me with that sumbitch overseer named Willis down the Blackwater to bury a metal box up in Pelican Bayou. He found a spot and had me dig a hole. Then I put the box in the hole and covered it up as he told me to. About that time, ol' man Willis comes at me with a knife. It came to me what had been planned for me when I saw the knife. So I threw a handful of dirt in his eyes and knocked the shit outta him with the shovel, then I threw him in the water. The gators down got him by now. Marse Ben, I'm in big trouble! I knew you was a good man and would help me if I could find you. Miz Berry told me that you was hid out in Yellow River Swamp, and I remembered the place you always liked to come when we fished down here."

"Caleb, I believe that under the circumstances, you would be justified in becoming a rich man." Ben smiled, and Caleb smiled back.

Caleb said, "Whatever's in that box must be pretty valuable to make it worth killing a $2,000 slave so he won't steal it."

"Caleb, ain't you overvaluing yourself a bit?" They both grinned.

Caleb then sat down at Ben's homemade table and attacked a plate of cold fried mullet and bread like a hungry bear would rip into a fresh kill.

While Ben watched Caleb eat, he asked, "Caleb, where did you get that nice butternut coat?"

It took Caleb about a minute to swallow enough food in his mouth to answer. "I borrowed it from Lieutenant Willis of the 'Federate army."

"Well, throw it in the fire and get rid of the ashes. I got another coat that you can wear. That butternut could get you hanged."

Ben knew that William Clayton was or had been, one of the richest men in the county before the war, and Willis was his overseer. Clayton had a large sawmill operation on the east side of Blackwater Bay. He also knew that his estate was named Cedar Grove and had been beautifully landscaped. Pelican Bayou was probably on his property.

"Caleb, after you rest awhile, let's go get that box because they'll come lookin' for Willis soon. Then we gonna get you and whatever's in that box out of here."

"Now, Marse Ben, I ain't wantin' to take nothin' that don't rightly belong to me," Caleb replied.

"Well, Caleb, we will just take what is fitting and proper for the services you have rendered to Clayton over the past . . . How long have you been working?"

"Since I was 'bout ten, I reckon. They started me out carrying water and lumber long about then."

"And you're around my age, ain't you? About forty?"

"Forty-two, I reckon," Caleb replied.

"So that's about thirty-two, thirty-three years. For working that long, especially for that son of a bitch Willis, that ought to be worth a thousand a year, don't you think?"

"Yassuh!"

At midnight, after Caleb had rested for a while, they set out in the skiff for Pelican Bayou. The night was illuminated by a full moon that seemed as bright as a street lamp. The stars were brilliantly alive, seeming to pulsate in the cold night sky. This facilitated the trip down the Yellow River, where overhanging tree limbs diminished visibility. When they reached Blackwater Bay, they turned north, moving as directly as possible up the bay toward the bayou. Ben and Caleb took turns rowing.

They reached the bayou in the early morning darkness, tired but watchful. After sliding the skiff quietly into the mouth of the bayou, they were hidden by sawgrass that formed a four-foot wall on each side. They sat listening for several minutes before deciding that they were alone. The unmistakable gleam from the eyes of several nearby alligators reflected in the moonlight. Ben used an oar as a push pole in the shallow water to glide silently farther up the channel. Suddenly, Caleb clenched Ben's shoulder, gasped, and pointed. In the moonlight, they could see what was left of Willis's severed head. It was devoid of all flesh and most of its hair but somehow retained one eye.

By the time dawn insinuated, they were well up the bayou that ran through a sea of sawgrass. Moving up the bayou, they reached a vast cypress tree that stood alone on the south bank. Caleb gestured toward the firm ground on which it stood. So Ben pushed the skiff in that direction. Caleb stepped ashore and secured the boat to one of the cypress knees protruding like stalagmites around them.

When both men were ashore, Caleb walked toward a thicket a few feet away. By tilting his head, he motioned for Ben to follow. Even in winter, the thicket was difficult to penetrate. Ben followed Caleb through it a couple of yards, where it opened into a small natural canopy. Ben saw where the sandy ground had been disturbed near the center of the thicket.

Ben concluded correctly that this was where Willis had Caleb bury the box. Caleb had brought the shovel he had earlier used to bury the metal box and dispatch Willis. He straight away began to dig while Ben served as the lookout. Neither man spoke as Caleb excavated, and the soft earth expedited the endeavor. In about twenty minutes, Caleb heaved the box from its hiding place to Ben standing above him.

"Caleb, stay quiet. I hear something!" he whispered.

By now, dawn had turned to sunrise. Darkness no longer provided its comforting cover, but at least the thicket concealed them. It also prevented them from seeing what they now heard. Coming from a few yards away on a sandy road, they heard horses, perhaps a dozen, moving toward them. Then the clopping sound of the horses stopped. They had reached the bayou a short distance upstream from Caleb and Ben, where a frail wooden bridge crossed the water.

"Sergeant Dollhausen, lead your men across the bridge," someone ordered.

Ben and Caleb lay still and quiet, trying to conjecture the scene from the sounds.

"Yes, sir," a voice replied.

"How the hell much farther to Yellow River?" There was no answer that Caleb and Ben could hear. Next, they listened to the unmistakable sound of hooves walking on wood. Walking the horses across the bridge took about five minutes. Then the sound of slow trotting resumed and gradually diminished to silence. Only the sounds of nature remained.

"Those were rebs," Ben said.

"Yes, sir," Caleb drawled. "And they weren't looking for Willis," Ben added.

"But I am," a high-pitched whiney voice behind them said. "Come out of there and bring that box with you."

They saw a man through the thicket. He looked well protected from the cold weather as well as from them. He wore a gray wool greatcoat and had a pistol pointed at them. A military-style brimmed hat pulled low in front obscured his face. Ben and Caleb could see a well-trimmed mustache and a prominent nose as they followed his orders and moved out of the thicket. "Now, it appears that I will have to find a different hiding place since I have no idea who knows about this one. Dear God, killing a slave is one thing. But I do hate it when I must kill a white man," the stranger said as he aimed and shot Ben in his right thigh.

Ben dropped to his knees, staring at the stranger defiantly, waiting for the coup de grâce, and it didn't come.

"I hope in time, sir, you recover from the wound," the stranger said to Ben. Ben knew instinctively that his demeanor after being shot somehow changed the man's mind about killing him. Whether it was sympathy or fear did not matter to Ben at the moment. "But that is in God's hands," the stranger continued. "Further, it is doubtful you will last long bleeding out with this weather. And I can't avoid the guilt I felt from the last man I killed."

The man who had suddenly taken on a major role in Caleb and Ben's adventure moved on to other matters.

"Now, Nigra, I will need you to rebury the box in a secure place while you tell me what happened to Lieutenant Willis. Afterward, your soul, if you have one, will go to meet its Maker."

Caleb lifted the box over his head and heaved it toward the bayou. The stranger, caught off guard, instinctively reached out to stop its flight. In that brief moment, Caleb drove his shoulder into the man and sent him backward into the cypress knees. Caleb and Ben both heard a crack like an axe splitting a log as the man's head hit a cypress knee and burst like a melon. Caleb heard the splash of the box in the water almost simultaneously, with the man's skull exploding. The man stared upward. His mouth lay open. Bloody saliva bubbles formed at the opening. He breathed with a gurgling noise for a few seconds, and then there was complete silence.

Caleb went to Ben, who, by this time, had sat down and leaned himself against a juniper. "He must have really scared you with that talk about meeting your Maker," Ben said and smiled.

"How bad are you hurt, Marse Ben?" Caleb said without smiling back.

"Actually, he almost missed me," Ben responded. The ball had missed his femur and major blood vessels and had merely pierced through leg meat. When Ben stood and dropped his pants and longjohns, Caleb could see the bullet just beneath the skin on the back of Ben's leg.

Caleb said, "I'll get it." He grabbed the projectile through the skin and yanked it out with his dirty fingernails.

"Shit!" Ben said through clenched teeth.

Caleb smiled his white-on-black smile and presented the ball to Ben.

"Souvenir," Caleb said.

They then turned their attention to their would-be nemesis. "Is he dead?" Ben asked Caleb.

"Well, he stopped breathing," Caleb replied.

"He's probably dead then," Ben said as if seriously ruminating about the question. "At least we got a hole to put him in. Let's see who he was," Ben continued. They started inspecting the body. But they stopped abruptly when they heard the rebel horses galloping back toward them again.

"They heard the gunshot. Let's get the dead man in that hole," whispered Ben. While he removed papers and valuables from the corpse and shoveled dirt over it, Caleb pushed the skiff deep into the marsh grass to lessen the chance that it would be discovered. They brushed the ground with juniper limbs to eliminate footprints. When they finished, they retreated into the deepest part of the thicket.

They heard the Confederates galloping toward them and the sound of horses finally crossing the dilapidated bridge. As before, Caleb and Ben had no view. Horse neighs, brays, and men's shouts showed that men and horses were on both sides of the bridge. To Ben and Caleb, it sounded like a disorganized search for the person who fired a gun minutes earlier. The two grew stiff and cold in their hiding place.

Suddenly, a lone dismounted Confederate soldier came toward their thicket. He was a thin boy who looked barely past puberty. Ben grabbed him, cupped his hand over the boy's mouth, and then pushed him to the ground. After Ben had the young soldier pinned, they made eye contact. The boy had tears in his eyes. He trembled with fear. Ben felt the warm wetness of the boy's urine where his own body lay over the boy's crotch.

This is who the older men send to fight their wars? Ben thought. He grimaced at the thought of killing the boy. In fact, he would surrender himself before he would sacrifice this child. Ben felt that he had a connection to this lad. Then he knew what it was. "Are you Irish, lad?" Ben whispered.

The boy nodded yes.

"Aye, so am I," Ben replied. "On your honor as a good Catholic, will you promise not to cry out if I remove my hand from your mouth?"

Again the boy nodded yes.

Caleb was nervously listening to this strange conversation. "Please quietly tell me what county you are from." Ben lifted his hand cautiously.

"County Kerry," the boy whispered.

"Aye, beautiful country," Ben said and smiled. "And what is your name?"

"Sean Bray," the boy whispered his reply.

"We mean you no harm, and we are fighting no one," Ben explained. "So if you promise not to betray us, I'll give you your life."

"Aye, I swear by the blessed Virgin Mother!" the boy responded.

"Thank you, Sean. And God keeps you safe. But, Sean, if you betray me, you will die and burn in hell for breaking your oath." The boy nodded again.

Ben let the boy rise to his feet and return to his unit. In a few minutes, the rebs were remounted and riding away.

Now that the troops had left, Ben disinterred the partly covered body and closed his eyes. He felt for the man's inside coat pocket and extracted his wallet. His personal papers showed that his name was not William but rather Thomas J. Clayton. So Ben assumed he was a brother, cousin, or uncle. He looked to be in his fifties, which ruled out a son or nephew.

Caleb dug Thomas a proper grave and reluctantly buried him in his greatcoat and the gold watch Ben found in his vest pocket, which would prove to be damning evidence if they were caught with them or any dead man's belongings. Ben dropped the man's hat down on his chest as an afterthought. Caleb covered him with dirt. Ben then stood beside the grave with his head bowed. Caleb followed Ben's lead and did the same.

Ben prayed, "Dear God, have mercy on this poor dead sinner and forgive Caleb for killing him. Amen."

Then Ben started to say the Lord's Prayer. Caleb joined in.

"Now we got to find that box," Ben declared when they finished the prayer. Caleb was already shedding his clothes.

"I know about where it went when I heaved it," Caleb said.

"Now, how could you know since you were rushing Clayton as soon as you tossed it?"

"Marse Ben, I know where I aimed to throw it."

Declaring that, he stripped off all his clothes, jumped into the water, and disappeared. When he came up, he had the box and smiled at Ben. Ben thought about how Caleb's dive in the cold bayou might make his body odor less intense. Caleb limped out of the water, shaking all over, teeth chattering. Ben thought he would like to have one of those picture-making machines to record Caleb in his state of near hypothermia as he retrieved the skiff and got him a blanket. Ben realized that he couldn't have a friend better than Caleb. Ben built a fire for him without regard to it being seen by the damned rebs or the damned Yankees. He gave Caleb a half cup of corn liquor to warm his insides. Caleb dried off and dressed by the fire while Ben opened a sack containing dried fish, bread, and honey. Caleb asked for more liquor to drink with his meal.

"Old Jack Tolbert sho' knows how to make white lightning," Ben said. "Maybe that will be my next venture."

Caleb expressed his thanks for Ben's generosity. They ate, drank, and moved quickly out of the bayou after Ben placed Clayton's box in the skiff's well.

They saw Clayton's boat near the mouth of the bayou. Ben pulled alongside for Caleb to collect items that might be of use to them. He also pushed the boat into the marsh grass to where it was difficult to see. Then Ben and Caleb headed for a large island in the river about where the bay began.

After quickly reaching the island, they hid the skiff in the thicket that covered most of the island, found a sandy spot, and rolled up in their bedrolls. As Caleb dropped off to sleep, his last thought was how bad Ben smelled. Ben did not fall asleep as soon as Caleb did. He was concerned about his hideout being discovered. The most practical thing for searchers was to stake out an area, watch for smoke, and listen for sounds of human activity. As Ben fell asleep, his last thought was of Amanda and how she managed to stay with her father in Milton.

CHAPTER 23

CLAYTON'S BOX: TRIP TO MILTON

Caleb woke as the sun was setting. He surveyed his surroundings. He then scanned the horizon. He saw smoke rising to the south in the direction of the Yellow River. He thought it was probably coming from the campfire of the rebels they had encountered earlier.

"Marse Ben," he quietly woke Ben, who was sleeping in a fetal position on a bed of pine needles. Ben roused and blinked his eyes.

"Look ayonder." Caleb pointed in the direction of the smoke rising vertically in the still air. Ben rubbed his eyes and sat up.

"We better avoid Yellow River for a while," Ben said. "Let's go to Milton. I've had Amanda and Jake on my mind. We can check on them while we are upriver this far. See how they're doin'."

"Marse Ben, we ain't looked in Clayton's box."

Ben smiled. "Yeah, we just might find a bunch of Confederate paper money and bonds in there. That wouldn't buy you a shot of whiskey after the war. It's pretty heavy, though. And it rattles like maybe there are some coins in there. Okay, Caleb, let's do it."

Caleb quickly retrieved the metal container, which was about the size of a cigar box and twice as deep. It was secured with a padlock. He disabled it with the shovel, removed the padlock, and handed the box to Ben. Ben waved him off. "You open it. It's yours now."

Caleb smiled and nervously opened it. He was dazzled by its contents. It was filled with gold coins and paper money from the United States of America. Ben and Caleb agreed that it totaled about $80,000. There were also some securities and deeds that Ben and Caleb had no interest in but were undoubted of much more value than the cash. "Let's take $100 apiece in small bills and coins and bury the box again. And, Caleb, I won't kill you after you bury it, in case you were wondering," Ben said, smiling.

When dusk turned to darkness, they started up Blackwater to Milton. The receding moon and stars provided adequate light for their passage. A short time later, they reached the burned-out wreckage of a wharf. They disembarked, hid the skiff under the wharf, and walked quietly up the street leading to Jacob Rucker's House. Fortunately, the dogs that had gone wild after being abandoned by their owners during the exodus to Alabama were scavenging elsewhere tonight. The night was silent.

When they reached the house, it was dark. Assuming that Jake and Amanda were asleep, they lay down in the unkempt yard and waited for daylight. After lying in the grass looking up at Amanda's bedroom window for perhaps an hour, Ben saw the light coming from her room and watched it move to Jake's room. *She was checking on him*, he thought. He heard about the problems Jacob had after the beating he took and about his long illness. But the light didn't stop in Jacob's room; it descended the stairs to the first level.

A moment later, the front door opened, and Amanda shouted into the darkness, "Who's out there?" She was holding the lamp and her father's rifle.

Ben quickly said, "Amanda, it's Ben."

Caleb jumped to his feet. Ben stood also. Amanda's shoulders went limp. She propped the rifle against the porch railing and said, "I thought the sawmills were up and running again. Somebody's snoring is awful!"

"It was Marse Ben," Caleb said immediately.

"Caleb, I was awake," Ben said. "I was so lost in thought that I wasn't even thinking about Caleb snoring."

"You both are probably guilty," Amanda said. "Come on in."

When Ben climbed the front steps, she wrapped her arms around him and kissed him on the lips. Ben responded with an intimate kiss, which she briefly returned. Ben smelled whiskey on her breath. She then greeted Caleb, who was a family friend. Once inside, Ben asked about Jake, afraid of the answer he would hear.

"He died a while back," she replied, holding back her emotions.

"I'm sorry, Manda." Ben embraced her again. "And I'm sorry I wasn't here," he said.

"You know, you shouldn't be here now. They'll conscript you or hang you if they catch you," Amanda said. "You shouldn't be here either, Caleb."

Caleb finally spoke again. "Miz Amanda, yo' daddy was good to me. He always be kind to me. He was a good man. I'm sorry he's gone."

Amanda thanked Caleb, and suddenly her tough facade disintegrated. She went limp and sobbed. Ben helped her to a chair while Caleb shut the front door.

"Daddy got better from the flu, and I thought things would get better. But then he started having terrible headaches. Nothin' would stop 'em. There's no doctor around here anymore, so I gave him all the remedies I could think of. I couldn't get opium for the pain. All I knew was to keep him knocked out with whiskey when Zeke could get it. I think he was stealin' most of it from the army. God bless him. Then about a month ago, Daddy was talking to me from the top of the stairs, tellin' me to get Zeke to find you and get me away from here for about the hundredth time, and suddenly he dropped over and fell down the stairs. He tumbled down so gently that I thought he was dead before he fell. Zeke and I buried him in the backyard the night he died so people wouldn't know. It was just Zeke and me now. Caleb, you know Zeke?"

"No, ma'am." Caleb shook his head. "Heard of 'im, though. He got yo' daddy to be his guardian. Zeke must be smart."

CHAPTER 24

ZEKE: CALEB'S PLAN

The dawn had arrived, and with it, Zeke came to the back door and knocked. After greetings all around, Zeke said, "Marse Ben, y'all couldn't have picked a worse time to pay a visit. All around Berryhill Road and the courthouse, rebels is swarmin' like bees. There must be two or three hundred of them, if not more!"

"Shit, oh, excuse me, Ms. Amanda! That means more scavenging. We have got to get out of here as soon as we can. And I mean all of us!" Ben said.

"Marse Ben, y'all may have to leave without me," Zeke announced. "I can't leave my woman here."

"We'll get her out too. We just need to come up with a plan. Where is she?"

"Well, I was surprised and happy to see her. She was made to go to Alabama with her owner, but he must have lent her to the rebels to work for them. She's up at the courthouse."

"How can you get her?" Ben asked.

"I can be as invisible as a panther when I have to be. I'll find her and bring her here tonight," Zeke said.

"Then we will get organized and leave tomorrow night," Caleb said. "There's a sloop hidden in the swamp up the river near Mortonia. The rebels missed it, and so far, the Yankees haven't found it either. I think I can slip up through the woods, bring it down tomorrow night, and run it down the east bank of the river. Y'all can float over to the mouth of Marquis Bayou in Zeke and Marse Ben's skiffs, and I'll pick you up there. If I don't show up by midnight, you go try to make it to the island off Pelican Bayou and hide until the Confederates clear out," he added.

"That's a great plan, Caleb! Maybe you are worth $2,000," Ben said. "Where's your whiskey, Manda? This calls for a toast to Caleb's brilliance!"

Amanda brought out a bottle and poured a generous portion into four dented tin cups.

"To Caleb! And to success!" Ben announced. They lifted their cups and toasted Caleb.

This egalitarian behavior made Caleb beam. "Let's hope it works," Caleb said modestly.

Zeke and Caleb departed, leaving Amanda and Ben alone. "Ben, you need a bath," Amanda said. "I'll fix you a washtub of warm water."

"OK, will you scrub my back?" he asked.

"No!" Amanda said emphatically. "You and Daddy were about the same size. Maybe you can put on some of his clean clothes."

She heated water in two iron pots which she hung over the fireplace, then poured them into a washtub when heated. She then carried the tub to a downstairs bedroom where she found Ben stripped down to his longjohns. After giving him soap, a towel, and a washcloth, she walked into the adjoining room. Ben stripped naked and bathed. The bath made him feel great.

"Look in the trunk by the bed and see if Daddy's things fit," Amanda shouted through the door.

He was pleasantly surprised to find that Jake's clothes fit him perfectly. "They fit!" he shouted back to Amanda.

"Good, I'm throwing the clothes you were wearing into the fire," she said. "Now, Ben, come out and let me see you."

Ben came into her presence, looking pleased with his appearance. He had even shaved.

"May I have another kiss?" he asked her.

"I would be honored," she responded, smiling.

They embraced and kissed intimately until she coyly withdrew. She could feel how much he was enjoying the experience. She led him to the back steps of the house where they could sit, concealed from the street. A dense canebrake and honeysuckle on the back fence protected the view of the backyard.

"I hate this war and what it has done to us," Amanda said quietly. "Daddy would be alive, and I trust that we would be married by now." Ben nodded his agreement.

"We are victims of the politicians," Amanda continued. "Lots of people around here didn't want secession. There would have been many more people against secession and the war if they could have foreseen what our own army would do to us."

"Well, the Yankees would have burned it all sooner or later. War gives a license for stealing and destroying," Ben said.

"I guess the Yankees were disappointed when they visited our house," Amanda continued. "The secessionists beat them to it. Zeke and I hid in the cane when we heard they were in town. I'm sure they wanted to find a piano for General Dow."

They both smiled.

"Amanda, I'm not going over to the Yankees, but that is the only way for you, Caleb, Zeke, and his woman," Ben said.

"I'm stayin' with you. I'd rather take my chances with you than get thrown in the middle of those Yankees who haven't seen a woman for months. If I'm gonna be ravished, I'd rather it be by you." She smiled and put her hand over her mouth. Ben smiled and kissed her.

CHAPTER 25

BEN'S TRIP FOR GUNS AND AMMUNITION

Ben helped Amanda gather food and other supplies that would be needed for the trip down the Blackwater. When night came, Ben set out to find rifles and ammunition superior to the musket he had been using since he went into hiding. He knew that he would have to be alert and cautious. He worried about barking dogs as he crept toward the Confederate bivouac wearing a CSA uniform Amanda had made from gray wool and the buttons from Jacob's U.S. Army days. But the dogs were interested in food scraps left along Berryhill Road, where the soldiers had dumped them. Ben could see the rebel tents and campfires through the leaves of azalea bushes bordering the courthouse. Some men were talking and laughing; others were telling stories. One was playing harmonica. Ben felt for them, knowing that they, like he, were victims of bad decisions by older men who didn't have to endure the dangers and hardships of the young boys they sent to fight.

As he watched, he became aware of the pickets walking the camp perimeter. He knew that if they caught him, he would be hanged or shot with little ceremony. The night was overcast, but a few yards away, he saw what he was looking for---a tent near the back of the encampment with two breech-loading rifles leaning against a nearby live oak tree. On the ground beneath the tree were accompanying ammunition pouches.

Ben was patient. He waited until the campfires died and most rebels had turned in for the night. He then walked directly into the camp to the courthouse well, filling two pails with water and picking up two dippers. He loaded them on a cart and walked back from the direction he had come. Quietly, he quickly picked up two rifles and ammo pouches by the tree and loaded them onto the cart. He shouted softly to the picket stationed on Berryhill Road posted in the direction of the river.

"Private, I'm supposed to take this to the pickets watching the river. What is the password so you won't shoot me when I come back?"

It was apparent to the picket that he had come from the encampment. "Away," the picket whispered.

"Thanks. I may stay and instruct them on what to look for. I'm familiar with how the Yankees try to slip up the river at night. I'll be back by daybreak," Ben said.

"What is your name, sir?" the private asked.

Ben said, "Lieutenant John Clanton. Colonel Clanton is my father." Clanton commanded all rebel troops in the area.

"Yes, sir," the private snapped to attention.

The big lie---it works every time, Ben thought.

Ben walked through the darkness, moving toward Amanda's house once he knew he was out of sight. In another twenty minutes, he was back at the house with his cart. He hid the rifles and ammunition pouches in the bamboo. He then made his way back to Berryhill Road and down to the pickets by the water.

As he approached, one of the pickets demanded, "Who goes there?"

"Lieutenant Clanton," Ben answered.

"Look," responded the picket.

"Away," Ben whispered. "I brought some fresh water. Is it quiet down here?"

"Yeah," the picket responded. "But about all we can do is listen. It's so dark."

"Why did you bring the water?" the shadow of the other picket asked.

"The colonel just wanted a report from the river, and he wants me to maintain my humility."

One of the pickets chuckled. The one who asked the question was nonplussed.

"The darkness makes you have to listen," Ben said, continuing his ruse, "and any sound travels a long way over the water. We got pickets at Bagdad too. The Yanks can't land a boat without making any noise.

And the Bagdad sentries would hear a steamer coming up the bay and alert us."

They spoke quietly for a few minutes, and then Ben took his leave. He walked up Berryhill and turned left when out of sight, returning to Amanda's house. *All that effort to get a couple of rifles and ammunition*, Ben thought to himself. He was exhausted!

CHAPTER 26

BEN SAVES AMANDA

Ben started to unlock the door from the back porch to enter the house when he saw that the windowpane by the door latch had been broken and the door was unlocked. He then heard a voice say, "Who gets to go first?" Another voice said, "I do, I seen her first, and it was me that figured out she was alone."

"Get at it then," the first voice said.

Ben quietly slipped off his boots and climbed the stairs to Amanda's bedroom without being seen. A lamp was lit in one corner of the room. What he saw sickened him. He quickly crept back downstairs and put his boots back on. He slammed the door as though he had just arrived and shouted, "This is Lieutenant Clanton. You men, get down here immediately!"

He heard a fumbling commotion upstairs as both men dressed and scrambled down the stairs. From the shadows, he yelled, "Attention!" Then he stepped out of the shadows and cut both men's throats before either man moved. They briefly stood at attention, spurting fountains of blood. Ben felt it hit his face and stepped back. The men crumpled to the floor in a messy pool of blood and urine.

Ben ran upstairs to Amanda. They had her stripped naked and tied over the ladder-back chair. She was gagged and unable to scream. He hurriedly wiped the blood off his knife and cut her free, untying the gag. As she stood up, Ben embraced her, never minding the nudity.

"Oh, Ben, thank you! Thank you! I love you!" she cried.

He held her for several minutes, trying fruitlessly not to think carnal thoughts during this serious moment. When she felt his hardness, she looked into his eyes and smiled. "I really tried not to," Ben said sheepishly.

"Well, I wasn't acting like a lady," Amanda said. She withdrew from his embrace and began to dress herself.

Ben, of course, excused himself. "Don't come downstairs until I tell you to. I got a mess to clean up," he said.

"Did you kill 'em?" she asked.

"I had no choice," Ben replied.

"I'm sorry," Amanda said.

"Well, looking at the bright side, neither one seemed like your type," Ben said jokingly.

"No, I like men with more teeth in the front and less tobacco juice in the corners of their mouth," Amanda said, continuing the morbid humor.

"Then I fall within your parameters?" Ben asked.

"Yes, and my man must go around with an erection all the time as you do," she teased.

"Why, Ms. Amanda, I am shocked at your indelicate language and your overly personal reference to my body!" Ben playfully responded.

He went downstairs and lit a lamp, keeping the wick down as low as possible. He carried the bodies of the soldiers into the bamboo and dug a shallow grave. He threw the bodies and his bloodied clothing into the hole after removing the personal effects from the two men and refilled the hole. He went back into the house and wiped up the great pool of blood from the floor. Then he called Amanda and asked her to mop the floor between the back door and the stairs.

"Okay," she said. "You can make sure I don't miss any spots."

When they finished, they took the food and supplies for the trip and went to hide in the canebrake.

CHAPTER 27

CELESTE, ESCAPE FROM MILTON

At the first light of morning, Zeke showed up with his woman, and Ben noted that she was quite a beauty! She was tall, slender, and the color of dark caramel. She was so winsomely lovely that it was difficult to avoid looking at her at every opportunity. Zeke was beaming when he introduced Ben and Amanda to her.

"Celeste, I'd like you to meet Miz Amanda and Marse Ben."

Celeste curtsied, her gleaming white smile expanding. Amanda opened her arms for a hug, and Celeste responded.

"Zeke has been tellin' me how nice you folks were!" Celeste said.

"Likewise," Amanda responded.

Ben said, "Zeke, you sure have excellent taste in women."

Celeste glowed with delight. Ben studied her. She wore a colorful yellow and red dress that fell right above the ankle. Her hair was short and nappy. She was barefoot in spite of the cool weather.

"I was a house servant before my owner got patriotic and lent me to Colonel Clanton," Celeste said. "His loss," she added, smiling big. "The colonel be taking a close watch over his soldiers around me. Don't want Marse to get mad 'bout anything happenin' to his best girl," she said innocently.

"Oh great!" Ben exclaimed. "I hope we have time to be gone before Clanton finds out you're missing. Who was your owner?"

"Marse Simpson," Celeste answered.

"How did Simpson treat you?" Ben asked.

"He treated all his folks good," Celeste said.

"I'm glad to hear that," Ben said.

"I still want to go with my man Zeke and get somewhere that we be free," Celeste told them, nodding her head thoughtfully.

Ben, Amanda, Celeste, and Zeke all slipped quietly into the canebrake to spend the day and evening before meeting Caleb on the river. The weather was now mild for January, and the sky was clear. Ben and Amanda lay on the ground between wool blankets, deep in the canebrake. Celeste and Zeke were serving as sentries. Celeste now wore boots that Amanda had given her to protect her feet. Ben was concerned about Celeste now being part of the group. He kept listening for hounds he feared would be brought in to search for her. He feared for himself, but his greatest fear was that Amanda would be caught with them. The slaves would be beaten, and Celeste would be returned to Simpson. He would be tied and executed. He did not know what they would do with Amanda. He was troubled all through the day they spent hiding and watching. He took advantage of the opportunity to be under a blanket with Amanda. His mind swung from fear to passion all day.

Finally, darkness settled over them. Amanda had fallen asleep on Ben's shoulder, and Ben awakened her. The four of them almost soundlessly made their way to the river. Celeste and Zeke got in Zeke's skiff. Ben and Amanda boarded Ben's. The Confederates on guard duty were upriver a hundred yards away, where a burned-out warehouse obstructed their view.

Almost effortlessly, they reached the meeting place, the mouth of Marquis Bayou. Ben and Zeke anchored just inside the narrow entrance to the bayou, across and slightly downstream from downtown Milton. Clouds rolled in, providing additional cover. Wrapped in blankets, they waited for Caleb and the sloop. Midnight came, and then at 1:00 a.m., Caleb had not arrived to rescue them. At 1:45, the wind changed from the southwest to the northwest and increased to twenty knots. The sky darkened. The group waited without openly expressing their apprehension, although inwardly, they were all wondering where Caleb was.

They heard a shot fired upriver, then a second one. Suddenly, they could see a white sail emerge from the velvety blackness. They heard more shots. The two sentries were quickly reloading the muzzles of their rifles and firing at Caleb. Ben retrieved his rifle and fired in the direction of the Confederate rifle flashes. Caleb reached the bayou and swung hard to port. He maneuvered the sloop in a circle inside the mouth of the bayou, hidden by tall marsh grass. The four new passengers quickly climbed aboard the sloop and grabbed their supplies from the now-abandoned skiffs. Then Caleb sailed out of the bayou downriver toward Blackwater Bay. Caleb knew they had to clear the last narrow section of the river before the Confederate cavalry could form and ride to the river's bank somewhere above Bagdad. The cavalry would have to travel no more than a mile from where they were encamped. A fusillade along the narrow section of the river would, no doubt, kill all on board.

The sloop was slowed by the added weight of the four additional passengers and their supplies. Caleb felt they were barely moving, although he knew better. Ben and Caleb's thoughts and concerns were almost identical. They had not heard a bugle---the wind continued to blow. Perhaps Clanton's men won't fire on Celeste. Who knows what might happen in the excitement? Suddenly, they heard the bugle. Ben had thought about ejecting the supplies to lighten the sloop but then reconsidered.

The sloop and its passengers were nearing the bay. Only one open riverbank north of Pond Creek was ideal for fusillade; the rest of the bank was swamp. Everything depended on who reached that place first. Ben and the others on board could hear the horses coming down Bagdad Road, which paralleled the river. Caleb glided the sloop past the open riverbank as the first riders came into the clearing. In the darkness, all the cavalry saw were the white sails of the sloop. Cavalrymen fired two shots, and both fell harmlessly behind them.

CHAPTER 28

CALEB SAILS FOR FORT PICKENS, BEN AND AMANDA HIDEOUT

Ben struck a match and looked at his watch. It was a little after 2:00 a.m. He knew the sloop had to head for Pensacola, Fort Pickens, or East Pass. He didn't know the situation at Pensacola, but East Pass was a dangerous and long trip. So he advised Caleb to take the others to Fort Pickens. He reasoned that it would be safer and more disciplined.

"Caleb, we have a matter to discuss," Ben said.

"Marse Ben, I'll write you, general delivery to Milton, after this war is over. Let you know where I am. I know you'll do right."

"Caleb," Ben continued, "if something happens to me, you know where to get what you need, right?"

"Yassuh," Caleb confirmed.

"Ben, I'm not going to Fort Pickens," Amanda spoke up. "I'm staying with you."

"You'll be safer at Fort Pickens," Ben said unconvincingly.

"I told you how I feel about that," Amanda said.

"Okay then, Caleb, drop us off at Pelican Bayou. We'll borrow the dead man's boat," Ben instructed.

"Yassuh, Marse Ben," Caleb answered.

"Caleb, you are a good sailor," Ben went on. "After you drop us at Pelican Bayou, head directly toward that distant shore. When you get a couple of hundred yards from land, turn west. Follow the coast until you reach the point. Go around the point and head southwest toward the end of Santa Rosa Island. That's where Fort Pickens is."

Ben drew a crude map with his knife on the floor of the sloop to help Caleb navigate.

"I have something else that might help." He pulled an old U.S. flag out of his supply sack. "If you encounter another boat, stay as far from it as possible. Zeke, don't fire unless fired upon. If you see a U.S. Navy vessel, run up the U.S. flag and this white handkerchief." Ben extracted his handkerchief from his back pocket and handed it to Caleb.

"If the patrol or the rebs approach you, try to get away," he continued. "Keep the guns under cover and use them only as a last resort."

Ben then handed a jug of water to Celeste. "This is all I can give you. Use it sparingly."

Caleb approached Pelican Bayou in the darkness. He furled the sails and coasted ashore south of the mouth of the bayou. Amanda and Ben quickly climbed ashore with their supplies. They groped about to keep from stepping in the wrong spot and falling. The openness of the water offered more illumination than the shadows of the tree-covered bank. Ben and Amanda, almost simultaneously, said goodbye to the three silhouettes in the sloop. "God keeps you safe," Amanda added. The silhouettes responded as Caleb pushed into deeper water and unfurled the sails. The strong wind continued.

Ben took Amanda by the hand and led her to high ground in a stand of young pines.

"We will stay here today. I'll find Clayton's boat, and then, we'll head for the swamp tonight."

They could have used the remaining morning darkness but were both exhausted. Ben spread a tarp on the ground and covered Amanda with blankets.

After she lay down on the tarp, she said, "Ben, I've needed a couple of ounces of whiskey to get to sleep since Daddy died."

There was an embarrassing quiver in her voice.

Ben got the jug and held it for her to drink. He then took the jug, replaced the cork, and sat it on the ground beside her. He lay down next to her.

"You've been through a lot," he gently told her.

Ben took the jug and took a good long draw for himself. They both were asleep in a few minutes, his body nestled against hers.

Amanda awoke at about 10:00 a.m. Ben was still beside her, but he was uncovered and still had his boots on. She could tell that he had been up awhile. "I got the skiff out of the deep water. It's hidden in the marsh grass," Ben told her. "I looked around and listened. If rebs were sent across Blackwater and down the east side of the bay, I couldn't hear or see them."

"That's good news!" Amanda replied. "I wonder what has happened to Caleb and his crew?"

"The wind is still strong, but now it's from the south, and it looks like rain. I think Caleb can handle the sloop as long as there is a breeze and not a hurricane. I imagine they are rolling on whitecaps right now," Ben said.

"I hope and pray they make it," Amanda said. Ben agreed.

They lay on the ground all day, talking quietly, kissing, and embracing one another. When night came, they quietly made their way south in the skiff. All was quiet at Ben's cabin. They cuddled together, but neither of them slept. The temperature was frigid. A cold front had moved in, and the weather was strange. The wind was again coming from the north. Temperatures that night dropped to the high twenties.

Ben looked around the cabin at daybreak. He saw no fresh horse tracks or footprints near the place, and it appeared nothing had been disturbed. *This place is practically invisible*, he thought to himself. He kept a close watch on the rebs half a mile down and across the river. They rode away from time to time, sometimes for several days, but they came back to this old campsite. He guessed they were hunting federal raiders, deserters, and Unionists. He was none of those.

But the rebs would lump him with the Unionists.

Amanda stayed with Ben at the cabin. Ben talked of returning to Ireland.

CHAPTER 29

AMANDA'S TRAGEDY

One night at Ben's cabin, Amanda snuggled up to him and said, "Ben, I must tell you something."
Ben said, "All right."
"I have a child. She is in Ireland with my relatives. My fiancé, Jean Paul, and I were deeply in love. We were in Paris, I remember, and it was a warm spring night. Chestnuts were booming. It was his birthday, and I was about to return from a visit to Ireland. We decided to stay in the Hotel Seine. We had adjoining rooms, and we made love. I got pregnant. When he left the hotel the next morning, he was shot in the hotel hallway. I opened the door to the hotel room to see the killer kneeling beside the body. I startled him. He looked up and then came toward the door. I closed and locked it. His face is burned in my memory.

"When I saw him leaving the hotel and walking toward a cafe, I quickly checked out of the hotel and took a room across the street in a hotel with a view of the Hotel Seine. I was grief-stricken but wanted to avoid a scandal. I sat by my window and saw the police come to the hotel. I saw them remove Jean Paul's body from the hotel. Then I sat and watched for the man who killed him to come looking for me at the hotel where he had killed Jean Paul, and he did.

"The next afternoon, I saw him enter the hotel carrying a traveling bag. It appeared that he wanted to have a good reason to be at the hotel if questioned. I knew he planned to kill me because I was the only witness and could identify him.

"Right after he checked in, I went over to the hotel and bribed the hotel clerk to give me his name and address. I could have called the police, but I was still trying to avoid scandal. And I'm sure my testimony alone would not convict him, especially the testimony of a woman with questionable morals, which would have been inferred by my being in the hotel with him without the benefit of marriage. One night of love, and I got pregnant. Can you believe it?"

Ben shook his head sympathetically.

"At the time, I thought the murderer had ruined my life forever and determined to get revenge. I continued to watch the hotel. The man left with his bag the next morning. I followed him to the station. Once again, through bribery, I found that he was going to the Port of Le Havre. So I guessed that he was sailing. I sent telegraphs to several shipping companies whose names I got from the hotel concierge. They replied, and one confirmed they had a gentleman by that name booked for passage to New Orleans. I surmised that he was returning to his home from New Orleans. Jean Paul and I were studying in Paris. When he was murdered, I lost interest in school. I was still bent on revenge. I returned to my home.

"A few weeks later, I knew I was pregnant. I had all of the symptoms. I told my grandmother the whole story, and she arranged for me to go to a convent until after the child was weaned. She is a beautiful little girl. The story at home is that our family took in an orphan. As far as I know, no one knows or knew the truth except my grandmother, my father, and now you. My brothers and sisters think I was still studying in Paris when I was in the convent. My mother, God rest her, dropped dead at fifty-five. My father, still grieving her death, wanted to try a geographical cure for his drinking and depression, and I wanted to track down the killer in America. His name is Thomas J. Clayton. Do you know him? I keep hearing about him but haven't seen him, and I'm sure it would surprise him to see me!" she said and then stopped talking because of Ben's look of surprise.

"What?" she asked. "What?"

"Did Mr. Clayton have a prominent nose and a thick mustache?"

"Yes," she exclaimed. "How did you know?"

"Caleb and I met him at Pelican Bayou. Caleb killed him," Ben said, still stunned. Ben told Amanda about what happened to Thomas at Pelican Bayou.

"I wonder why he didn't kill you like he did to Jean Paul," Amanda said. "Thomas must have had a guilty conscience having killed a white man. But he had no such conscience about killing a black man, and I think he thought I was badly wounded and would die in the cold." Ben continued.

"This is all so strange," Amanda said. Ben nodded in agreement.

Amanda suddenly tensed. "Ben, I'm not the woman you thought I was. I'm sorry I misled you. I'm not pure like you thought," Amanda said.

"Were there other men?" Ben asked, nervous about the answer.

"No, Jean Paul was the only one ever, and I loved him dearly."

"I wanted to ascertain that my standard of sexual inequality remains comfortably in place," Ben said jokingly.

"Do you think less of me?" Amanda asked.

"Actually, I think more highly of you. I have no doubt that you would have shot Clayton between the eyes if you had found him. He's a lucky man to have avoided you!"

"I think not." Amanda smiled.

"Why did Clayton kill Jean Paul, do you suppose?" Ben asked.

"Jean Paul was at a reception for a political candidate and overheard Clayton, who worked for his brother, and another government official discussing overbilling the French government for yellow pine lumber sales. At the time, Jean Paul feigned no knowledge of English, and he told me all about it. When Clayton learned later that Jean Paul was fluent in English, he panicked and came looking for him."

"Perhaps you can rest now," Ben said.

Amanda held Ben close and wept for both joy and sorrow. "So, Ben, I'm more nervous about sex than I was before, and I can't go home pregnant again."

"Then marry me now," Ben said.

"Maybe we can see if the rebs have a chaplain," Amanda joked.

"No, at the first opportunity, I mean," Ben said.

"Ben, you've already proposed once," she reminded him.

"I know, but we didn't set a date. And that date would be as soon as possible!" Ben said.

Later, she fell asleep in his arms, feeling safe and loved. Ben decided that night that they would stay put until the war ended. He felt certain about the outcome. The industry of the North would eventually prevail. After the war was over, they would go back to Ireland. Ben opened a locket Amanda wore around her neck. Inside was the image of a little girl---Amanda's daughter. He observed that the child bore a striking resemblance to the child who appeared in his dream. Milton and the rest of Santa Rosa County would be no place for Amanda, himself, and the Unionists after the war. He believed that Celeste, Zeke, and Caleb were safe. Caleb knew where Clayton's box was buried and could retrieve it after the war.

CHAPTER 30

BEN'S VIEWPOINT

Ben was bitter about the Confederate abandonment and destruction of everything that provided a living for most of the people of Pensacola, Milton, and the rest of the surrounding area. He believed that General Bragg could have taken Fort Pickens with the rumored five thousand Confederate troops he had in Pensacola. This would have made Pensacola another port for blockade running, using the new railroad to transport cotton and lumber in exchange for military and other supplies and equipment the South needed so urgently. On the other hand, perhaps the rebels could have left at least 1,500 well-equipped men to defend Pensacola while making it appear that there were more. And why could they not have built more frigates to protect the Pensacola Bay area instead of destroying the two ships under construction in Milton?

Further, his contempt for Lincoln was just as great as that for the secessionists. All the Southerners wanted was to drive the Union military out of the South and be left alone to follow their belief in states' rights, preserve their financial investments in their labor force, and prevent the freed slaves from terrorizing the Southern whites. Was it right for Lincoln to force his form of government on the Southern states at the cost of hundreds of thousands of lives? Southerners did not believe Lincoln would pay the price in human lives to force an unconstitutional concept of a strong central government on the seceded states.

Ben had recently also been thinking of his friend John Smith. He had fished, hunted, drunk, and gone to church with John. Since Ben went into hiding, he had not seen John. Ben knew John was working for the Southern cause in some capacity. He knew how John thought, and he was always helping the underdog even when he had a somewhat different view. John probably knew that the Southerners just wanted to control their own destiny and were against an overly powerful central government. John would think that slavery was not a big issue with the majority of Southerners who owned no slaves, except for the problem of what to do with them or how to control them. He would have known there was little, if any, criticism of slavery in the Bible as interpreted by Southern churches.

CHAPTER 31

YANKEE RACISM

As Ben was thinking of getting John's help, he was shocked and surprised to see Caleb, Zeke, and Celeste scratching their way up from the river.

"Mornin', Marse Ben," Caleb said like he was casually walking past Ben in Milton.

"Mornin' y'all," Ben replied nonchalantly, adding, "what happened?"

"Yankees just started shooting at us from the shore at Fort Pickens. When they saw we were just a bunch of black folks, they thought it would be fun to use us for target practice," Caleb explained. "We didn't know nothin' to do but turn around and try to get back here."

"Those SOBs that have come to end slavery are just as racist as they say we are."

"Zeke took one through the shoulder," Caleb said.

Ben looked at Zeke but couldn't help first glancing at Celeste. She had used her colorful dress to bandage Zeke's wound. Her sleeves and skirt, up to her knees, were gone. Zeke and Celeste were walking together a few feet behind Caleb. Zeke would have looked comical, wrapped in Celeste's clothing, except for his appearance. He was pale, and the bullet wound appeared to be more severe than Caleb thought. It was closer to his heart than his shoulder.

CHAPTER 32

SISTER ALICE

"Celeste, this wound is very bad. You did a good job stopping the bleeding, but he still lost a lot of blood."

Celeste leaned over Ben, who was kneeling by Zeke. She took Ben by the shoulders and said, "We got to get Sister Alice down on the sound. She be able to save his life."

Celeste was so desirable it made Ben nervous for her to be in his space. After questioning Celeste further, Ben learned that Sister Alice was a Creek Indian woman of middle age who lived dangerously close to Camp Walton. The locals referred to her as "Wise One" or "Wise Healer" because she had healed many people, some of whom he knew personally. As Ben was considering stealing a horse from the rebs, which would have been extremely difficult and risky, what seemed a miracle occurred.

Caleb had walked to the road to reconnoiter and met an Indian woman who seemed to be communing with the spirit world, seeking direction. Caleb was her answer. Caleb told her what had happened. She smiled a smile of faith and peace and followed Caleb to Ben's cabin, where Zeke lay on the only bed. Sister Alice and Celeste cleaned Zeke up. Then using Ben's moonshine whiskey, abundantly for his pain and the wound, Sister Alice removed the slug and cleaned the wound. She did not know why she poured the whiskey into the wound. She just knew that it worked on healing. Celeste redressed the wound. Zeke was cooperative and only uttered a sound when Alice reached in with clean hands and probed for and removed the slug. Zeke was hurting badly but finally slept.

Alice sent Caleb, Celeste, Ben, and Amanda to look for plants she described to them in detail. Ben was amazed at the plants she knew. She took the plants and began to make a medicine for Zeke, which smelled earthy. Then she ordered everyone out of the cabin. Alice stayed with Zeke for five days, denying herself food and drinking little water. She hypnotized him for hours, planting healing thoughts in his mind. On the evening of the fifth day, Alice declared Zeke healed (and sometime later, Celeste said the scar had gone away). "Wise One" left at sundown to return to the sound. She did not want their praise because she knew she was only a conduit for the Great Spirit.

CHAPTER 33

BEN FINDS JOHN

As soon as Zeke was out of danger, Ben headed to Milton to try to find John Smith. Ben crept around Milton, looking for someone to talk to. The streets were washed out badly and grown up with weeds. The buildings not burned were boarded up. It smelled burned, with a bit of an animal smell.

Having no luck in Milton, he began the mile-long walk to Bagdad. Just after he left Milton, he encountered a small group of blacks fishing. They all stood up when Ben approached. "Howdy, Marse. Can we help you?" This translated to, "Man, are you crazy? What the hell are you doin' here? Are you a deserter?"

"Howdy, men." Ben never used the degrading "boy" that was often used by white Southerners when addressing blacks, regardless of age. Ben continued. "Do any of you men know where Mr. John Smith stays?"

"He layin' low right now. He stays gone a lot. White folks say he fixin' to leave again, don't know where." The volunteer news reporter was the same man, "Snowball," whom Ben had met the day of the Confederate destruction.

John could not bear to stay in his house in Milton. He was too lonely without Maria. He didn't like to cook for one, so he moved into the boardinghouse.

When Snowball was convinced that Ben was John's close friend, he called him aside and told him where John was. Snowball led him to a large house off Oak Street. Ben decided it was a well-disguised boardinghouse. The windows were boarded up and covered with curtains. They entered through the rear path with a canopy of wild grapevines and honeysuckle hiding it from the street. People knew that those with horses should put them in the corral about a quarter of a mile away and cautiously approach the house.

It was suppertime when Snowball left Ben at the rear door of the boardinghouse. When Ben entered the dining room, everyone stopped eating and looked at him. John immediately recognized him, stood up, and said in his unique way, "It's all right. This is my trusted friend, Ben."

Nobody said hello; they just went back to eating. After small talk between John and Ben, they withdrew to John's room.

CHAPTER 34

THE REST OF JOHN'S STORY

John told Ben all about his blockade running. "When I realized the Confederate army was deserting us and they burned every damn thing we had to make a living, I decided that I was going to try to recoup my losses from the same jackasses who ruined me and get lots of the rebels' gold or foreign currency like French francs, English pounds, or even U.S. dollars further to relieve my hurt bank account and my hurt feelings. And since I am from Great Britain, I am looked upon as a brave friend of this new nation. And the first time they try to pay me in Confederate currency, the price is going up tenfold. Further, I will get rid of it as soon as possible. Or I may refuse it outright, depending on how the war is going. The South can't win this war. And the states like Mississippi, Alabama, and Georgia are going to turn into 'Africa North' when the slaves are freed." John went silent for a few seconds, and Ben was about to make a comment, but John was just resting his voice for a moment.

"It's a good thing I had the *Carolina* at sea when the Confederates attacked themselves. They would have been stupid enough to destroy it!" Ben had given up on talking, so he just nodded in agreement.

John continued speaking about blockade running. He brought out a bottle of bourbon and poured three fingers into each glass before he began again. This obviously pleased Ben immensely since he consumed his drink in one gulp.

John gave him a refill while he was talking. "I studied all the factors I could imagine that would affect making a successful run. These included phases of the moon, wind patterns at different times of the year, ever-changing patterns of the shifting sand near the bar, and changes in the primary sand formation of the west end of the island. The island, dubbed Santa Rosa, is nothing more than a giant sandbar," John concluded.

Unfortunately for John, he had to check some of these possibilities on a regular basis. A collapse of a wall of sand near the bar could slow the *Carolina* or cause her to run aground. None of these events occurred, but it was prudent to go down and inspect the area below.

John would put on Union pants, a cap, boots, and suspenders, but no jacket. Bare-chested, he would come around the south side of the island rowing his skiff, take off his clothes, and start making dives along the bar. Nobody questioned him. He was in and out of the water numerous times. He used a pencil and notebook to record his findings. By evening, his inspection was complete. He would give a copy of his report to the NCO in charge and ask him to post it. Then he would return to his skiff and row away. John's temerity reflected his nerves of steel.

CHAPTER 35

HERNANDO LOPEZ, JOSE GARCIA

After John talked about running the blockade for too long, he let Ben vent for a while about his situation. Then John told him the story of Maria. John told Ben that when he learned about her old husband being kidnapped and that Jose Garcia was probably involved, he sent Oliver to Malaga to hire a private detective to assist them.

Michael Mendoza, a man in his middle sixties, proved to be a good choice. He was able to determine that Garcia was the head of a ring of bandits, pirates, smugglers, and kidnappers that operated primarily in the western Mediterranean.

After his encounter with John in the Gambia, he retired from slave trading and came back to his native Spain. Michael learned that Garcia had a villa in Ronda, two blocks from Maria. Hernando Lopez, Maria's husband, was sitting in Garcia's house, too weak to leave.

When John found out where Garcia lived, he went to his villa. He carried two concealed pistols and a knife. When he knocked, a black maid opened the door. "May I help you?" she said with a pretty, youthful white-toothed smile.

"Yes, is Señor Garcia in?" John answered.

"Yes, who shall I say is calling?"

"John," he said. "He will know."

"Please come in," the maid said, thinking John was an old close friend. "And please sit down," she added.

John had Oliver stationed at the back door. John sat with his back to the wall in Garcia's exquisite villa. Jose Garcia entered the room wearing a smoking jacket, obviously containing a weapon.

"John, how is the shoulder?"

"Quite well, thank you," John answered.

"It is good to see you," Garcia lied.

"You seem to have changed your operations," John said.

"Yes, I primarily do purchasing, shipping, and sales."

"How many ships do you have now?"

"Only four," Jose answered.

"How many do you have harbored here?"

Jose was getting nervous, irritated, and curious.

"Three. Why do you ask?" Jose inquired.

"Those screw-driven steamers?"

"Yes, damn it, why?"

"I have only my *Carolina*," John said. "I'm going to sink 'em."

"Why?" Garcia asked.

"Cause Señora Lopez can't pay the ransom."

Jose Garcia sat quietly for a full minute. "I will let Lopez go if you will not go to the police and will not sink my ships."

At that point, Garcia started to retrieve his pistols. But John had a sharp knife to his throat before he could retrieve the pistols.

John said, "Remove your jacket with the weapons left inside."

Garcia complied. His neck was hurting from the pressure of the knife. "All right, damn it!" Jose shouted.

John simultaneously pulled out his pistol and removed the knife from Garcia's neck. Oliver came in the back door when Jose shouted, and he found Señor Lopez in an adjoining room, sitting silently.

"I'm sure Jose has paid off the local police. Help me find something to tie him up with." They took Jose Garcia, tied and gagged, and then Señor Lopez to the Lopez house. Later that evening, they took Garcia in Maria's carriage to the *Carolina*. That night, drawing a huge crowd, they located and fired their cannons at Garcia's ships below the waterline with impunity. All ships sank after an hour of cannon fire. John, Maria, Oliver, Señor Lopez, and their prisoner, Jose, sailed for England on the Carolina. Oliver took Garcia to the Royal headquarters to be charged with slave trading, piracy, and kidnapping. John took Maria away for a while with Señor Lopez's permission.

As they strolled across the Thames River, John asked, "Have you really waited all this time for me?"

She smiled and said, "Well, yes and no."

He understood that she had reached satisfaction with perhaps more than one or two men, as they had done together back in Pensacola. But she had never had intercourse.

"Others have touched me with their hands, and I have reciprocated. I almost did once, but . . ." She stopped in midsentence. "What about you, John?"

"Here's the hotel," John replied. The question was never mentioned again in all the years they lived.

When John and Maria entered the hotel, he signed the register as Mr. and Mrs. John Smith. The room was elegantly appointed with soft cotton sheets on a canopy bed. They had both bathed on the ship. She had worn a fur coat for the foggy London air. He had worn a Confederate admiral's uniform as a novelty, knowing it would be out of style soon. As John removed his uniform, he noticed Maria opening a travel bag with a low-cut yellow dress in it and matching shoes. John removed the rest of his clothes and put on a robe. His curiosity mounted as she proceeded toward him in her fur coat. When she was a few feet from him, she slipped off her shoes and dropped her fur coat. There, she stood wearing the same white peasant blouse and red skirt she had worn the night they met. She was as beautiful a sight to John as she was the first time!

She looked at John and said, "Let's start over."

The rest is history. They made love for a week and started a line of descendants with the misfortune of being named Smith.

Since the British were neutral in the War Between the States, no hostility was allowed there. John was wearing his Confederate uniform when he and Maria left the hotel. He stopped a bobby to ask directions. As he was listening to the bobby, who carried only a nightstick, three very drunk Union sailors approached them. One fat, red-faced, intoxicated Union sailor came up to Maria, put his arm around her, and said so John could hear, "I'd like to have my way with this little Southern whore."

John calmly asked the bobby, "He touched her. Isn't that assault and disorderly conduct?"

"Yes," the bobby said.

"May I borrow your stick?" John asked.

"Well, ahh . . . yes," said the bobby.

John took the stick and popped the Union sailor between the legs. The fat Yankee fell to the ground. The other two drunken Union sailors, having come straight from a pub, made the mistake of coming after John. The one on the left, a tall, lanky fellow, charged. John struck him on his throat. He fell gagging. The third, he poked in the solar plexus, causing him to tumble. Thus, all three were immobilized within fifteen seconds. While they were down, John pulled his sharp sword, cut all their suspenders, and quickly removed their trousers. He handed the stick back to the bobby, who was speechless! John thanked him and then threw the trousers over the limbs in a nearby tree. Unruffled, he took Maria's hand and walked away. Behind him, he heard the crowd that had gathered applauding. Then someone started singing "Dixie," and all the Londoners joined in, not doing very well with the words.

When they returned to the *Carolina* to meet Oliver and Señor Lopez, only Oliver met them. "Señor Lopez is dying," Oliver said. Señor Lopez lay on a bunk. Oliver had done all he could. He had called in a physician who gave him the message. The doctor had told Oliver to keep him as comfortable as possible. He gave him some opium and told him how much to give. Oliver had even called in a Roman Catholic priest to administer the last rites.

Maria went to him. He was barely conscious, but when he saw her, he smiled. "Maria," he whispered, "I am happy for you, and I wish I had been the right man for you. You brought joy to my heart, and I only brought you trouble."

"No, old man, I love you," she said. "You taught me much about my heritage and my culture. You taught me how to be a Spanish lady. I will always remember and love you."

"Goodbye, my little girl," he said.

With that, he closed his eyes and did not open them again.

There was a slight smile on his now-dead lips.

Maria, John, Oliver, and the crew sailed for Cuba, where he planned to leave Maria until the war ended. He intended to visit her when he ran the blockade. Señor Lopez was buried at sea.

"And where and when after Havana would you like to go?" John said when he had finished his story. His voice startled Ben, who flinched when John raised his voice. Ben was almost napping as the story wound down. Fortunately, John was looking out the window and not at Ben.

Ben thought about John's question. "I just want to get away from those cursed Yankees and the idiots that burned everything of mine and my friends. It'll take ten or more years to get things running again, and things will never be the same," Ben replied.

"I read in a Havana newspaper that Confederates have been invited by the Brazilian government to come there. The emperor wants us to come to grow cotton after we lose this stupid war," John said.

"That beats being treated like prisoners by Yankee boys. And what about the safety of our women from Nigras and Yankees after the war?" Ben said.

"It might be a good way to make money, transporting Southerners to Brazil. Yes, whites and Nigras!" John got excited. "I'll look into it. But first, I have some business with Mr. Clayton. Clayton bought off the military by paying the Confederate government enough to dress, equip, and feed a company of men. He, of course, was in the militia, which did little but hunted down deserters who were sick of the disgusting killing and knew the cause had long been lost, probably beginning at Gettysburg in July of 1863," John declared.

"The heroism of the Confederate army we hear of elsewhere has not reached the poorly led and undertrained troops down here. It seems they have been outsmarted and routed by Union troops every time they skirmish," Ben added.

"The Confederacy is dying. It has been divided into enclaves of resistance. When Richmond falls, that will be the end. There are too many Yankees and embittered rebs here. Let's leave as soon as possible. Yes, maybe Clayton's loss of his treasure will be sufficient punishment," John added.

CHAPTER 36

MATT AND MARK: ACCUMULATING TRADE GOODS

While John and his Mexican crew were running the blockade out of Pensacola Bay, Matt and Mark were spending their time accumulating and hiding cotton and lumber while avoiding the Yankee patrols. They were also executing contracts with the Confederate states to acquire supplies and armaments. They insisted that Confederate funds be paid in advance, including a sizable profit. Further, they asked for gold at the current exchange rate to the Confederate currency. To have asked for U.S. currency would have been rude and was never suggested. Though the price seemed high, it was reasonable.

In most cases, the lumbermen and the few planters had stopped building up inventories. They didn't know whether the Union would take it or the Confederacy would burn it. Many of the farmers grew vegetables and raised livestock to feed their families or to barter for other necessities. Because Matt and Mark were Canadians, they were not subject to Confederate conscription. But with the war going badly for the South and the rate of desertion running high, there was a general disregard for this legal nicety.

People from the Florida Panhandle and South Alabama would stop them when they were on the way to pick up what the Union called contraband, that being cotton and lumber from isolated sawmills: "Why ain't you boys somewhere killing Yankees? Are you yella? Are you deserters?"

Matt would give a sarcastic answer in reply. The Hanshaw brothers finally bought pistols in case they were attacked.

On one memorable outing, when questioned by a Confederate major, Matt replied, "We are helping the great lost cause." This angered the major because it hit on the truth.

"Arrest these men!" he ordered.

Matt spoke. "Arrest us, and you will have to borrow gunpowder from the Union. We are going to lead a few wagons down to Milton to load the contents on the *Carolina*. They are then gonna run the blockade, God willing."

"Order withdrawn. How do we know you are telling the truth?" said the major.

"Lord knows we can't carry much, but under a thin layer of hay strung together to make a mat, we got room for some lumber or cotton. When the next wagonload of hay comes down the road, check it. But please keep that to yourself. We are Canadian, not subject to conscription, but we do more than a dozen foot soldiers," Matt said as Mark nodded his head.

The major said nothing for a few moments and then said, "I have heard rumors of a ship that can run the blockade."

Matt and Mark produced personal documents that showed them to be Canadian citizens. "Perhaps we can provide escort services, and your wagons could travel in a convoy."

"That would be great," Matt responded to the Major.

"Very well," the major replied.

The major, Franklin Skinner, said, "I have fifty men. I'll send ten to inform the wagons strung out to tighten things up to run a convoy." The ten were selected and began moving north toward Alabama. In a few minutes, one came riding back with troubling news. The private who was sent back to report to the major was nervous.

"Sir, Major, sir." His voice trembled. "Yes, Private," the major answered.

"We have received reports that there are Union troops of company strength moving east from Chumuckla. They are mounted and may already be in the area."

"Good job, Private," the major said. The private beamed. "They probably came up the river road after a quiet ride across the bay," Mark said.

"We will send two scouts, one south and one southwest, to ride about two hours, staying under cover when possible. If you encounter them, try to lead them to the West Coldwater or the Little Juniper Creek crossings. We will have men at both crossings to attempt an ambush," the major ordered.

Mark thought how useless all this effort was, considering that the war was almost over. He thought John might not return with the needed military supplies until after the South had surrendered. He wondered if Florida could have stayed in the Union and declared its sovereign right of neutrality in the conflict. *Lincoln was a real ass,* Mark thought. If the North wanted one thing and the South wanted something else, was it worth the lives of several hundred thousand mothers' sons to prove? Let the Africans fight their own battle. They would have to eventually.

After Major Skinner and his militia departed to try to set up ambush points, Mark and Matt were locating and congregating the wagons along the roads toward south Santa Rosa County. When they had accumulated twelve wagons and were moving south, three Union squads came over the hill from behind them. Apparently, part of the Union company had followed the river road to an area north of them. Matt and Mark had anticipated such an event, so every wagon quickly flew a U.S. flag, and the brothers had purloined Union uniforms for such an occasion.

Before the Yankees were near enough to see, Matt asked Patrick McCaghren, an adventurous thirty-year-old Tennessean who loved excitement and challenges, and two other men to act as snipers. They rode in three directions to find suitable positions.

Mark had also laid hands on Union letterhead stationery on which he had written a requisition for ten thousand bales of hay. It was signed by an anonymous aid to a Union officer in an illegible handwriting. Mark ran toward the captain of the Union company as they approached. After saluting and saying "Private Hanshaw," Mark said, "Thank God you are finally here!"

The captain looked confused and said, "What are you talking about?"

Mark then continued. "A courier named Corporal Jordan sent this message." He handed it to the captain, who said, "I'm Captain Johnson."

The captain studied the note, which read,

Any officer(s) presently on reconnaissance in the area north of Milton: Please escort and protect the hay wagons to Milton. You are relieved to return to regular duties thereafter.

It was initialed illegibly at the bottom and was not dated.

Matt had to join in. "There are a couple of squads of rebels in this area. They have been sniping us and killed three of our escorts. Guess they figure that is the easiest way. Maybe you should warn your men, sir."

"I'll give my own orders, son," said the captain.

Captain Johnson carried on a five-minute conversation with his sergeant before a shot rang out. The sergeant fell from his horse with a bullet through his head. Matt looked at the captain and sadly shook his head. Another second, and the captain took a slug through his neck. Blood spurted like a fountain from the captain. For a fleeting moment, Matt, briefly seeing the captain sitting dead on his horse, thought he did, indeed, look like a grotesque fountain statue. He fell from his horse and lay on his back, his head turned sideways, the spurting blood giving him his second baptism. Matt, afraid he might be mistaken for a Yankee, squatted behind a wagon. Matt had the hymn "Washed in the Blood" on his mind for a couple of days, occasionally humming it unconsciously.

Matt ordered the wagons to move. They started fording a small creek.

A second lieutenant rode up to Matt and a Union corporal who was near him. He shouted, "Corporal, have the troops take cover and tell them to keep their heads down! Send ten spread out and undercover to find those snipers."

"I am in charge of all these soldiers now, that is unless I get shot. My name is Ken Smith," the second lieutenant said.

"Matt Hanshaw," he said as he extended his hand and shook Smith's hand.

Smith, who liked to talk, said, "I got this great idea to come down from Prince Edward Island and become a U.S. citizen. As soon as I was naturalized in Philadelphia, a man in a blue military uniform came by with a form that already had my name on it, and I knew I had to sign. So now I am the commanding officer of a little piece of the U.S.

Army when I was actually planning on moving to Texas. I'll go after the snipers." He reluctantly rode away.

Lieutenant Smith rode in a large semicircle to the area approximately behind where one of the snipers would be. That is where Smith found the sniper at the foot of a huge magnolia with lots of climbing limbs. The sniper was Patrick. He was smoking a cigar while leaning against the tree. Patrick and Ken looked at each other. Ken smiled first. He said to Patrick, "War is silly as hell. Why should I shoot you? I don't even know you. You ever been to Texas?"

"No, but I've always wanted to," Patrick replied. "There are lots of lands, and I hear those Mexican senoritas are beautiful, willing, and plentiful.

"You got a horse?" Smith asked.

"Yes, up that draw. You?" Patrick asked.

"Yeah," said Smith. "You won't shoot me, will you?" Smith added.

"No, let's make a blood oath," Patrick said as he cut the palm of his right hand enough to draw blood. Ken did likewise. They grasped bloody right hands.

Smith said, "By mixing our blood, we swear we will not harm one another, and we will protect one another to the best of our ability, so help us, God."

Patrick said, "I affirm my concurrence with this oath."

They rode away that very day. GTT (Gone to Texas) was carved on the sniper's magnolia tree.

The Union corporal, with the disappearance of Ken Smith (assumed missing in action) and the captain and sergeant dead, was the highest-ranked Union soldier. So he was in charge.

The corporal and the Union squads, minus eight killed by snipers, escorted the Hanshaw convoy to Berryhill Street in Milton. From there, the Union soldiers went back north. The Hanshaws saw to it that the trade goods made it to the *Carolina*.

The Union soldiers on the way from Chumuckla never appeared. So Major Skinner and the rebels saw no action that day. But the major laughed out loud when he heard that Union troops escorted the Confederate convoy!

CHAPTER 37

CHARLES W. WARE

Charles W. Ware, a retired U.S. Navy captain who had helped in the attack of the *Bedford* and *Dorsett*, was now a planter with only a few hundred acres and five slaves in north Santa Rosa County. His land had been clear-cut and burned. Mr. Ware had planted the soil with various experimental crops such as peanuts, corn, grasses, and other crops to determine what worked best in rotation with cotton to overcome the acidity and other harmful effects of growing cotton where yellow pines had stood for thousands of years. The clear-cut areas were mostly barren of all but yellow pine seedlings. But Charles Ware was determined to grow cotton. He lived on the money he got from the timber sale. Ware was a pioneer of sorts in Santa Rosa County, trying to grow cotton because the emphasis had been on harvesting the bountiful virgin forests and manufacturing lumber and wood products.

Over time, Charles had finally begun to grow marketable cotton, but then the War Between the States began, and his two sons, David and Russ, had gone to fight for the Confederacy. So everything Charles had done, except learning to grow cotton, was useless because of the Union blockade and his sons being gone. He eventually had little cash, and they lived off the food they grew themselves, fish and venison.

Charles was unable to pay three years of property taxes on the land and improvements. So he was thinking of selling the slaves, but only on the basis that they remain together and be treated well. Before that could happen, the Claytons paid the taxes in hopes that they could acquire the land for taxes owed by Charles Ware.

Charles was a religious man who accepted the Southern cultural custom of slavery. He thought, like other Southerners, that this was proper based on the Holy Scripture. He went to church on Sunday and took his family and slaves with him. The slaves sat upstairs. He treated his slaves well and saw no wrong in what he was doing. His Baptist preacher thought it was a nonissue. Social mores were set in stone.

John invited Charles Ware to come with them to Brazil. He was the type of person John wanted, and John insisted that once in Brazil, the slaves would be freed.

Mr. Ware agreed to his proposal knowing the war was lost and that he could not repay the property taxes the Clayton family paid to possess his land eventually. He believed he could grow cotton on land recently cleared of old-growth forests in Brazil because of his experience. After Mr. Ware agreed to go to Brazil, John paid Ware's property tax so Clayton would not get his property.

On the Ware plantation, the slaves were treated more like employees and family than slaves. The slaves and Ware's children played together when they were young. An illness among the slaves was treated almost as seriously as an illness in the Ware family. The Ware children were taught not to look down on the blacks and to treat them with kindness. This increased productivity, but now, all he could grow was food for the family and slaves.

After Charles committed to going to Brazil, John told Charles he had paid the property tax Charles owed, plus an estimated amount for two additional years. This way, David and Russ, if they survived the war, could either farm the land or sell it and join their father in Brazil. The Claytons were going to be disappointed.

John appointed Charles Ware as chief of operations of the Brazil project.

CHAPTER 38

GOING TO BRAZIL: WILLIAM CLAYTON'S SUICIDE

When he sailed, John had human cargo rather than cotton or lumber. Caleb, Zeke, Celeste, Oliver, Matt, Mark, Ben, Amanda, and John were accompanied by a select group of whites of like mind who would be harassed by both the Yankees and secessionists. In addition, many blacks who were loyal to their former owners and wanted to escape the prejudice that would follow the war were on board. Among them were Snowball and other freed slaves. John, Ben, and Oliver had gone to Pollard, Sparta, and Brooklyn, Alabama, on horseback to talk with the slaves and sometimes their owners. These were people who fled the Florida Panhandle when the Union troops took Pensacola. John and Ben had made a list of those, black and white, that they wanted to invite---mistreated slaves, separated black families, certain compassionate slave owners who were good cotton growers, and their equally competent former slaves. They completed their task in two hard-riding sorties. Their imaginations were fired at the thought of going to Brazil. John reserved the right to deny passage to anyone who had a reputation for mistreating slaves or allowing an overseer to do so.

While they were in Sparta, John encountered William Clayton, who conspired to have Caleb killed by Willis. John asked him about a slave of his named Caleb. Clayton arrogantly said that he had so many slaves he certainly didn't know their names.

"They are just Nigras," he said.

Ben then came over to take part in the discussion. "How is Thomas these days?" Ben asked.

William Clayton looked puzzled. "Thomas is fine," he lied. "How do you know him?"

"We had a talk once. Then he shot me," Ben said. "He was a compassionate man. He didn't shoot me but once."

"Was?" William questioned.

"Yes," Ben said. "Listen, you sent your overseer, Willis, with Caleb to bury something on Pelican Bayou high ground. You ordered Willis to kill Caleb after he buried the box. Instead, Caleb killed Willis in self-defense. Then you sent Thomas to find Willis. Instead, Thomas found Caleb and me. Thomas was going to finish the job Willis was sent to do. Again, Caleb killed in self-defense."

"You can't prove that," William said angrily.

"Thomas confessed everything before he died. He said you gave the orders," Ben bluffed.

"Okay, I gave the orders. He was just a Nigra," William said again, with arrogance.

"Mr. Clayton, the times are changing," Ben declared.

"Where is the box?" William asked.

"Buried somewhere, I suspect."

"I have lost everything because of this war," William said. "Including my youngest brother."

His shoulders were slumped as he slowly walked away. He stopped after about ten steps, withdrew a small pistol, put a slug in his brain, and then dropped into the dusty road.

Over the next several days, slaves and owners alike created an exodus of substantial proportions. Then word came that Richmond had fallen and General Lee had surrendered. The best news was that the Union blockade had been lifted. John persuaded other shipwrights and previous ship financiers to construct an additional ship to carry the overflow from John's ship.

Maria's uncle, Señor Moreno, had gone to Havana to be with Maria for a few months. He was financially sound. He liquidated his landholdings early before the war started and invested in U.S. bonds by way of Spain. Additionally, he invested in the shipbuilding project.

They thought they could sail the *Carolina* out of the bay and into the gulf without difficulty, but there were still Union ships in the area. The *Carolina* was built in England and was 201 feet long, and 26 feet wide, with a draft of only 9 1/2 feet. She had two screw propellers and two stacks burning black bituminous Alabama coal. As she sailed out of the bay, one of the Union ships followed her. As soon as John was aware that they were being signaled to stop, John ordered the steam engine to full speed. The Union ship exposed her cannons. The *Carolina* suddenly lunged forward, leaving the Union ship in the wake. She left the captain of the Union ship scratching his head. The *Carolina* was a quarter mile ahead.

It took them several weeks to reach Brazil because they stopped in Havana and stayed a few days to pick up Maria and her uncle. There was almost a spirit of camaraderie between the blacks and whites because they had broken the bonds of conventionality and social structure by making such an unheard-of decision to go to Brazil.

Of course, John and Ben's vision of a more compassionate society, segregated but just, was a far different vision than that of the diehard white supremacists who wanted to rebuild the Old South elsewhere as it had been before.

A few days after reaching Havana, Amanda and Ben sailed to Ireland on a private vessel, the *Panama Queen*, to pick up Kelly, Amanda's daughter, and bring her to live with them in Brazil.

John, who had corresponded with his family over the years, knew that Anne, his now-grown sister, had not yet married. He also learned from Anne that his father, Abraham, had died. A major stroke took him after he had been retired a short time. So John's mother, Virginia, and Anne joined them in Dublin. After Ginger lost Abraham, she easily accepted the fact that he would not be coming home every six months or so. She knew he loved her, but she could not help but notice the new lovemaking techniques he practiced on her when he came home. She never asked him about it. In fact, she rather liked it and wished her two male friends were as proficient.

Of course, Ginger had general guilt over her lifestyle. But she simultaneously enjoyed it. A lot of the fun went out of her iconoclastic behavior when Abraham died, and she no longer felt that she was getting even for his womanizing. So when John offered her a chance to start a new life in Brazil, she was thrilled.

Ginger met Michael upon his arrival in Brazil to visit. He had been honored and decorated in a special ceremony by the U.S. government for his service. It was love at first sight, and they married a few months later.

John Geoghegan's sister, Anne, had decided to stay in Britain. She had much to lose by leaving. Anne had been given considerable attention by the sons of wealthy landowners and even some of the more free spirits within the aristocracy. She picked Charles Winton from among those who had proposed to her. He was an excellent choice. Winton was a decorated career naval officer who came from an eminent English family whose tradition was to serve in the Royal British Navy. Two of his ancestors had been knighted. The highest levels of the British government sought the advice of the Wintons. So Anne stayed with Winton.

Many ships carrying Southern cotton growers anxious to start over in Brazil assembled off the coast. They included the *Carolina,* who led the modest fleet. John and Maria were happy to be together on this new adventure. A cannon shot was fired from shore to signal the ship to enter the harbor. The ships were all decorated and flew the stars and bars. A Brazilian band played "Dixie," and crowds were cheering.

It was as though they were the conquering heroes!

EPILOGUE

It is only a legend, or more like a myth, conjured by proud, vanquished people. It is barely ever spoken of anymore. It is still passed down by a few ancient sons of sons of sons of the supposed witnesses. It has passed orally, to be told as though it bears some unstated, unknown, great significance.

On that stormy Halloween night, when the *Carolina* was aground and in grave peril, Union infantrymen were being loaded into Boston whalers to attack her while she was in the shallows. Suddenly, a rebel yell rang out, and someone shouted, "Kill 'em, kill 'em all!" And a mere squad of "grays" on horseback broke into the company of Maine infantry boarding the boats. After the storm, a full moon lit the fog that rolled over the combatants. The rebel swords glowed like silver scythes, cutting wheat as the Union soldiers fell, slashed, dismembered, or almost beheaded. This massacre occurred while the Spaniards attacked the Union gunboat, killed the crew, and set the ship ablaze.

Uncounted Union soldiers fell. A few escaped by swimming far from shore. The rebels gave no quarter. Another rebel yell rang out from the leader of the grays, this time from the throat and spirit of Colonel "Fighting Joe" Ray. But there is a strange twist to the story. Colonel Ray, a courageous battlefield leader who came from Jones Valley in the foothills of North Central Alabama, was killed at Gettysburg in Pickett's Charge on July 3, 1863. Nevertheless, he talked briefly with the rebs after the action at Pensacola, after which he rode away with his men in gray.

Perhaps to somewhere that we have never been.

www.ingramcontent.com/pod-product-compliance
Lightning Source LLC
LaVergne TN
LVHW040152080526
838202LV00042B/3128